★

The logical move would have been to get the hell out of there, and fast. I've never been noted for my logic. I couldn't see a damn thing, but I could hear someone moving in that back room, and the curtains shifted as Nick's body was dragged through. I shouted, "Hold it!" and lunged forward, still clutching the .38 without taking it out of my purse.

Whoever was holding Nick dropped him with a thud. A door slammed. I dragged the curtains open. Nick was sprawled on the battered wooden floor at my feet. There was a body on the couch. A woman's body. Very dead. There was no one else in the room, and no windows, unless they were covered up by the crimson-and-gold wall hangings. I ran for the door, but it was locked from the other side. Nick was half-conscious and moving some. I checked the woman on the couch to make sure my initial assumption was correct. It was.

★

Through the Eyes of the Dead

Melisa C. Michaels

WORLDWIDE.

TORONTO • NEW YORK • LONDON
AMSTERDAM • PARIS • SYDNEY • HAMBURG
STOCKHOLM • ATHENS • TOKYO • MILAN
MADRID • WARSAW • BUDAPEST • AUCKLAND

THROUGH THE EYES OF THE DEAD

A Worldwide Mystery/December 2000

Published by arrangement with Walker Publishing Company, Inc.

ISBN 0-373-26370-8

Printed in U.S.A.

THROUGH THE EYES OF THE DEAD

ONE

THE FIRST TIME I saw Nick he was trying to steal my car. In broad daylight, mind you. And he would have succeeded, if it hadn't been for the minor fact that I had the rotor arm from the distributor in my purse. I keep my car shiny clean, no dents, the upholstery in good repair, so how was he to know it wouldn't start no matter how good he was at hotwiring anything with an engine?

It was one of those July afternoons when the hot inland winds blow the smog out of the blue enamel sky and across the bay, and the air is acrid with distant forest fires and dry grass waiting to burn. I was wearing the most backless of my backless dresses, my lightest sandals, and no underwear, and I still felt overdressed. My skirt clung to the back of my legs where I'd been sitting down. My hair, completely undone by the heat and the wind, clung in damp, curled strings to the back of my neck.

I had spent the afternoon sitting in a broiling office staring out the open windows with unbridled lust at the distant white triangles of sailboats on the bay. The roof of the building next to the office was coated in some silver substance that reflected heat like an oven. Beyond the sailboats, San Francisco's pastel skyline had shimmered gently in the brilliant summer light, a magic place beyond reach of beating sun and harsh reality. I wanted a tall, icy gin collins. And I wanted to be one of the Beautiful People, or the boat owners, or whatever the hell it takes to get a July weekday afternoon out on the water with nothing more pressing to worry about than whether you're wearing enough sunscreen lotion.

Instead, I got to worry about where my partner was, how our current case (notice I didn't use the plural; that wasn't an oversight, it was a damned shame) was proceeding and how we were going to pay the rent. After eight hours of that I left the office with a headache and only a vague concern over whether it would make any difference in the immediate future that there was no way to conceal a .38 revolver under a backless and nearly frontless dress. I had to carry the thing in my purse, where it seemed to weigh about ten pounds and wouldn't be easy to reach if I needed it. My major concern was where I could find the nearest gin collins, with lots of ice.

The only parking place I'd been able to find that morning was two blocks from the office. It didn't seem too bad in the cool of the morning, but two blocks were two too many in the scorching afternoon sun. Then, when I got there, I found this wild-eyed lummox trying to hot-wire my cherished 1973 Capri.

He tried to look casual about it, as if he'd lost his keys or something. The parking lot was full of cars, and there was nothing to tell him that I belonged to that particular Capri, so he took a chance. When he saw me looking at him he grinned, shrugged, and tried the engine again.

"Got a problem?" I asked, reaching for the rotor arm in my purse. My fingers closed first on the .38, but I pushed it aside. There were a lot of people around, so I didn't feel particularly threatened by an attractive, well-dressed car thief, even if he should turn surly.

"Won't start," he said. "Must be out of gas." He just sat there, in the driver's seat of my little red Capri, and smiled through the open window at me with such incredible innocence I nearly checked the license plate to make sure I hadn't made a mistake.

Instead, I pulled the rotor arm out of my purse and showed it to him. "This might be part of the problem," I said.

He glanced at it and back at me. His face was young and tanned and oddly handsome in a gaunt, high-cheekboned way. His eyes were shadowed, the irises so dark they looked almost black. For just an instant, when he realized it was my car he was trying to steal, there was a look in them as wild and trapped and desperate as a bird with a broken wing. Then it died and his expression went flat, lifeless. "This your car?" he asked.

"Sure is," I said. "And if you'll kindly pop the hood and then get out of it, I'll put the rotor arm back in and drive it cheerfully out of your life. Steal somebody else's car, buddy. I'm not in the mood."

I don't know what reaction I expected, but not the one I got. He popped the hood, climbed out of the car, and closed the door to lean against it, watching me as casually as if we were old friends chance-met on the way home from work. "Couldja give me a ride, then?" he asked. "Just to Oakland? It's real important, you understand. I gotta get there right away."

I stared. "You sure as hell have nerve."

He flashed the kind of sweet, disarming grin that always reminds me of puppies and little boys. "I know."

Well, that was it. I didn't know why, and I sure as hell knew it was stupid, but I was going to give him a ride. By way of token resistance I told him there was a BART station right down the street.

He shrugged. "I got no money."

I put the distributor cap back on and closed the hood. "I'll give you BART fare to Oakland. It's not a lot."

He watched me a moment, judging. "No, thanks." He turned away. "I'll steal another car."

"Get in," I said.

He wasn't surprised. He was already on the way around my car to the passenger side before I finished speaking. "Hey, thanks," he said. "That's real nice of you. You must be a very good person. This is a true kindness—"

"Don't overdo it." I got in and started the car. "Fasten your seat belt, or the damn thing will buzz at us all the way to Oakland."

"I could fix that for you," he said.

"So could I, but I happen to think seat belts are a good idea. Fasten yours."

He fastened it and leaned back in his seat with an easy grace. I could tell he didn't like the seat belt. There was a poised readiness about him, as if at any moment he might explode into action—or flight—and the seat belt made him feel trapped. It showed. But he didn't argue.

"Where to?" I asked.

For some reason, that startled him. He recovered quickly, but there was something there.... I was, by this time, thoroughly curious about my mild-mannered, well-dressed, dark-eyed car thief. My work brings me into contact with all kinds of people, but this was a new breed. He was expensively dressed in a dark suit, nicely tailored, a sleek silk shirt, and brown leather dress boots. He talked like a street kid, possibly (if Bruce Springsteen's mangled diphthongs were any guide) from New Jersey. And he had tried to steal my car.

"I, you understand, I don't know exactly the address," he said, "but I can tell you how to get there. It's, um, it's on San Pablo Avenue."

"Okay, we'll start from there." I pulled out of the lot and into sporadic traffic on Berkeley Way, turned right on Shattuck, and again on University, heading for San Pablo. The interior of the Capri, which had been baking in the sun all day, was stifling even with the windows wide open. The steering wheel was almost too hot to handle, and the upholstery glued itself instantly to my unprotected back, presumably with sweat, though it felt more as though the plastic had melted against my skin. I could think of nothing I wanted less to do than to drive a stranger to Oakland when I could be finding something cold to drink.

"What's your name?" he said. "I'm Nicholas."

"Pleased to meet you, Nicholas. I'm Aileen."

"That's a pretty name. Aileen. That's got a nice sound to it. What you do, are you a secretary or something? I never met no secretary that knew nothing about car engines." His voice was sweet, almost musical. The combination of rough accent and gentle voice was oddly charming.

"I'm a private investigator," I said.

He glanced at me. It wasn't the usual "What's a pretty girl like you doing in a line of work like that'' look. I couldn't read it. "You mean like on television? You're a private eye like on television?''

I managed not to laugh. "I mean like on television. Only it ain't like that. The P.I. business in real life is mostly slow and stolid and just about as exciting as driving a garbage truck. We repossess a lot of cars for the Bank of America. That sort of thing.''

"I'm surprised,'' he said. "What you look like, you look like you're maybe a secretary or…something.''

"Thanks…I guess.''

"Oh, I don't mean nothing, I mean,'' he said. He was so flustered, I did laugh, then.

"It's okay,'' I said. "And what d'you do? When you're not stealing cars?''

"Me? I'm, um.'' He glanced at me sideways, and I knew that whatever he said, it was going to be a lie. Or at least it was not going to be the whole truth. "Well, I'm a, I do some, um, black-topping,'' he said.

"What, like on streets?''

"Usually driveways. For nice places, the driveways of rich people….'' He caught me staring and let his voice trail off uncertainly.

"Are you for real?'' I looked at his hands. They were clean and soft, with long, sensitive fingers and not a speck of tar under the nails. "Either that's an outright lie or you're working one of the oldest scams in the business. Which is it? Paint thinner and crankcase oil, or you're into something else that leaves your hands clean and your conscience dirty?''

He glanced guiltily at his hands and sighed. "Paint thinner and crankcase oil.''

It's one of the oldest scams in the business. A couple of guys drive around ritzy neighborhoods claiming they work for a regular contractor but they don't mind making a little extra on the side, and they'll be happy to resurface your driveway for ten percent of what a regular contractor would charge. The sucker gets a nice, shiny layer of paint thinner and crankcase oil on his driveway that washes away in the next rain.

"Only I don't exactly do that, anymore,'' said Nicholas. "And anyway, what d'you expect? It's just my dumb Gypsy ways. I don't know nothing else.''

"C'mon. Any idiot can find *some* honest way of making a living.''

He shrugged, possibly embarrassed. "Not a Gypsy. That ain't our way.''

"You're saying you really *are* a Gypsy? It's not just a figure of speech?''

"I don't understand that, 'figure of speech.' I'm a Gypsy, sure.''

"Sure. Okay, it makes a colorful story, Nicholas."

"Nick. You could call me Nick."

"And that makes a convenient change of subject, Nick."

We drove in silence for a while. Now that we were out on the main streets, traffic was moderately heavy, and nobody was in a good mood. Bay Area residents don't react well to what we refer to as "heat waves"—two or more consecutive days of temperatures as high as eighty or even eight-five degrees. We like our summers foggy and cold. But the Pacific High was on a rampage that summer. The temperature rose all the way to ninety, and it stayed there. To someone from most other parts of the country that might not sound very hot, but to residents of an area where the mean temperature, summer or winter, is about sixty-four degrees Fahrenheit, it's *very* hot. The parching wind kept the air clean, blowing our pollution off somewhere to the southwest and scattering it, and the sky was deep, glossy, incredible blue. And people were fainting in the streets from heat exhaustion.

They were also driving in the streets the way suburban women push shopping carts at the local market. It's a method I refer to as "Look out, damn you!" Or sometimes, "Ooops!" Put an ordinarily pleasant, mild-mannered, reasonably polite individual of either sex behind the handlebar of a shopping cart or the wheel of a car, and suddenly that individual's personal space requirement extends seventeen feet in every direction, and anyone who infringes on it is The Enemy. The only rules I've ever discovered to this game are those found in any game of chicken: whose car is biggest, newest, fastest; who can turn on a dime and who can't; who's willing to sustain minor damage and who isn't; and who can shout the worst curses in a crisis. These are the guidelines.

I discovered that Nick was pretty good at curses, though I didn't understand half of what he shouted when a wrinkled Volvo full of teenagers tried, in the interest of making a left turn across two lanes of traffic, to kill us that afternoon. His tone and his upraised fist were self-explanatory even if the words were incomprehensible. The teenagers changed their minds about the left turn and Nick settled back in his seat with a look of infinite satisfaction.

"What language was that?" I asked. "It sure worked."

"Romany," he said. "We got good curses."

"Romany?"

"Gypsy," he said.

"Oh, right. I forgot."

"You don't believe that, do you, that I'm a Gypsy."

"Should I?"

"You want me to tell your fortune?"

"No, thanks." I smiled at the notion.

He decided the smile meant we were friends, I guess. "We're almost there," he said. "Hey, Aileen?"

"Yeah?"

"When we get there," he said, and hesitated, and started again. "You understand, I gotta go here because my sister Lela, she called me, she's thirteen years old and my father who is an evil man has sold her to a boy she doesn't like. You know. Not that it would matter only this boy, he's seventeen years old, which anybody can see is too old for Lela, and besides, already he's beat up on her twice—"

"Stop," I said.

He stopped.

"You're obviously going to ask me for something," I said. "I think we should get something straight first."

He waited, watching me.

"When you want something from me, you don't give me a wild story, and you don't try to guilt me into it, and you don't try to bribe me or any other damn thing. You must ask. Then I say yes or no, and we're done with it. Okay?"

He thought about it. "There," he said, pointing. "It's up there in the next block. But you maybe won't be able to park on San Pablo. Try a side street."

I tried a side street. "Explain to me, in simple terms I can understand, why it is I'm parking? Why I'm not just dropping you off in front of your destination and going on my merry way, which is to find the nearest gin collins, with ice?" I wasn't looking at him; I was looking for a parking place. Don't ask me why.

"You don't want a story, am I right?"

"You're right." I turned a corner, starting around the block, still looking for a parking place.

"I just ask?" It was clearly an alien concept.

"You just ask."

"Would you come into the *ofisa* with me?" It came out fast and scared. That's why I was looking for a parking place. I've always been a sucker for lost kittens and wounded birds.

"Would I come into the *what* with you?"

"The *ofisa*, that's a fortune-telling place. My sister, she has an *ofisa* here."

"Your thirteen-year-old sister?"

"My other sister."

I found a parking place. It was tight, but that was another thing I liked about my old Capri. It might be built like an orange crate (that's what my brake man told me, and who was I to deny him his images?), but it fit in little parking spaces. "All right," I said. "What for?"

"You're a *gadjo*," he said.

"I'm a what?"

"A *gadjo*. That's a person such as yourself who is not a Gypsy. Maybe it don't matter but sometimes my family, they're more friendly in front of *gadje*. But I should tell you, if my father is there—"

I interrupted him. "No stories, Nick. I'll accept the warning, for what it's worth, but not the story. And I think I should tell *you,* if this is some weird kind of setup—I don't know what it could be, but whatever—I'm not quite the innocent and defenseless mark I might look like."

We were out of the car by then, and I'd removed the rotor arm from the distributor and was putting the cap back on. "You don't look defenseless," he said. "Aren't you gonna lock the car?"

"Why should I? It won't start, and there's nothing valuable in it. If I lock it, somebody'll break the windows to get in. If I don't, what can happen?"

He wasn't interested in my logic, or in my car; his mind was already ahead of us, in his sister's *ofisa.* "Okay, then let's go," he said.

I put the rotor arm in my purse and wondered briefly why I was following this self-proclaimed Gypsy into of all silly places a fortune-telling joint, on an errand that was possibly hazardous, probably illegal, and certainly none of my business.

He glanced back to see whether I was coming. His eyes had that wild, dangerous look again. At the same time he seemed oddly vulnerable, like a frightened child. Life would be boring with no mysteries. I followed him.

TWO

IT WAS A scummy neighborhood, and the unaccustomed heat wasn't helping matters any. Oakland was usually warmer than Berkeley by four or five degrees, because in Berkeley we got cold winds straight off the ocean, through the Golden Gate, that Oakland didn't get. Even so, they were no more used to real heat than we were.

In the rich neighborhoods, up in the hills, people were probably escaping the afternoon sun in their kidney-shaped swimming pools and cool, walled gardens. Down here in the heart of the city there were no such convenient refuges. After five o'clock the heat was beginning to let up, but it was still oppressive, and it would stay that way at least until the sun went down.

Porches and tenement stairways were lined with overweight men in tee shirts and gaunt women in tattered cotton dresses with curlers in their hair, all sipping beers from sweating cans and swatting absently at flies. Neighborhood youth, who would ordinarily have been about their rightful business of stealing hubcaps or a little casual shoplifting—it was too early in the day for mugging—were gathered in weary droves on street corners, laughing and talking too loudly and showing off a lot of sunburned, sweating skin. The air reeked of dog shit and ripe garbage.

Nick led me around the block to San Pablo, apparently oblivious to the squalor around us. I followed him warily. If I'd known I was going anywhere besides the office today, I would have selected a more demure dress. This was not a neighborhood in which I really wanted to attract attention. At work, sure; many a male client who might have left when he realized both detectives in the firm were women had stayed when he saw what we looked like. Not because men think attractive women capable of better P.I. work; they think the opposite. But they seldom think clearly at all in Sharon's presence, and I'm pleased to say that a lot of them like extra opportunities to look at me too. Still, near downtown Oakland I would rather have been looked at less.

The storefronts in this neighborhood were as shoddy as everything else. We passed a narrow pawn shop with two rusted toasters and a broken-necked guitar in the window; a hardware store with windows so full of dusty, jumbled items I couldn't pick out any to name; and a doorway that said simply MASSAGE in garish purple letters on the burlap-curtained window.

The next shop turned out to be Nick's *"ofisa."*

There was a big pasteboard sign in front that said Madame Sonja in red script lettering and underneath announced partial details of Madame Sonja's rather remarkable powers. Over the doorway another pasteboard sign, this one taped to the inside of the transom window, was painted to represent three playing cards. In the front window, which was heavily curtained in lace and a strange gold-threaded paisley-patterned fabric, a small sign affixed to the glass by means of a clear plastic suction cup indicated that the place was open for business.

"This is it," said Nick, in case I entertained any doubts.

I entertained doubts, but not as to the identification of the storefront. "Are you sure you want—" But he already had the door open and before I could finish speaking he caught my hand to pull me inside with him. I clutched my purse and waited for my eyes to adjust to the candle-lit dimness within.

Nick released me as soon as we were inside, and shut the door behind us. An invisible bell tinkled merrily with each movement of the door. All I could see were candles and curtains. When the bell stopped its tinny clinking, everything was deathly still with that waiting silence that always means a safe is about to fall on somebody's head. The room was miserably hot and stuffy, laden with the stink of sandalwood incense, and even without the sense of impending doom, five minutes in there would have given me a terminal case of the willies.

"Sonja?" Nick moved cautiously into the room, calling out in a half-whisper, as if the unnamed tension in the air had touched him, too. "Lela?" The candles flickered in the air currents created by his movement. There was no other response.

He moved through swimming shadows toward the curtains at the back of the room, his steps silent and careful. I stayed where I was, one hand clutching the cold comfort of the .38 in my purse, watching the darkness. I couldn't hear anything but my own heart beating, and the muffled sounds of traffic outside. The incense was already giving me a headache. He parted the curtains and a brilliant shaft of artificial light stabbed through.

I had at first thought this was a small room, its walls hung with curtains. Now I saw it was long and narrow, divided in two by curtains across the center. In the unexpected light I saw Nick pause, heard him exclaim in alarm or fear, and then something hit him and he went down. The curtains closed, dropping the front half of the room back into flicking dimness.

The logical move would have been to get the hell out of there, and fast. I've never been noted for my logic. I couldn't see a damn thing, but I could hear someone moving in that back room, and the curtains shifted as Nick's body was dragged through.

I shouted, "Hold it!" and lunged forward, still clutching the .38 without taking it out of my purse.

Whoever was holding Nick dropped him with a thud. Before I got the curtains open I heard a muttered curse and someone running. A door slammed. I dragged the curtains open, using one hand and one shoulder so I could keep the other hand in my purse, clutching the .38. Nick was sprawled on the battered wooden floor at my feet, beside a worn velvet overstuffed couch whose clawed front leg was tangled in the hem of the curtains.

There was a body on the couch. A woman's body. Very dead. There was no one else in the room, and no windows, unless they were covered up by the crimson and gold wall hangings. I ran for the door, but it was locked from the other side. Nick was half-conscious and moving some. I checked the woman on the couch to make sure my initial assumption was correct. It was. Then I bent over Nick, who was trying feebly to sit up.

"Lie still," I said. "You're hurt."

He ignored me. "Lela," he said, and struggled up. His face was awful. Whoever hit him had given him a good clip, leaving the hair behind his right ear matted with blood, but it wasn't that kind of pain that twisted his expression. It was the utter desolation of some terrible loss. I didn't understand, until he reached for the woman on the couch, what it was.

"That's not your little sister," I said.

He realized it even as I spoke. The blow to his head had left him confused and unsteady, but he was recovering quickly. The woman on the couch was a good many years older than thirteen, though she was small and slim and with her face turned away she could easily be mistaken for a child.

Nick sat back and covered his face. His hands were unsteady. "Oh, jeez," he said. "I thought he'd…" He let the sentence trail off and looked up at me. "We better get out of here." His mood could change quicker than a cat's. I wasn't sure I was following it. He'd gone in the space of thirty seconds from horror to relief to sudden fear, and I didn't know what he was frightened of.

"We'd better call the cops, is what we'd better do," I said, the voice of sweet reason…or so I thought.

He stood up, and had to catch my arm for support. "You don't understand." He got his balance and stood for a brief instant staring down at the dead woman, then looked at me. "We gotta run."

"D'you know that woman?"

"C'mon." He started for the door.

"That's locked from the outside. D'you know this woman? Where's the telephone?"

"Over there." He caught my arm before I could move in the direction indicated. "Aileen, you don't call the cops. We gotta get outta here. What you don't understand about Gypsies, they'll call the cops, you know, they'll tell the cops I did it, that I killed her. Maybe even they'll say you were here. That'd make sense, since how else can they say…they'll say they saw us. That they saw us kill her. We gotta run.''

''That'll just make it look like we really did kill her. Nick, it's our word against theirs, even if you're right. And we can prove we weren't here whenever this woman was killed. We were in Berkeley.''

''For that, you got witnesses?''

''Sure…I don't know… It's according to when…''

''We don't know when. And what you said, our word against theirs, that ain't good enough. What you don't understand, there'll be fifty of them to say they was here and they *saw* us. We gotta *go!*''

We might have argued till the cops came in, but Nick wasn't having any. His mind was made up. All of a sudden the mild-mannered, soft-spoken gentleman I'd been with for the last hour disappeared. When I made no move to follow him his face went stiff and so dangerous that I said involuntarily, ''Nick?'' and backed away.

''*Gajende,*'' he said softly, in a voice gone cold and deadly. He whirled away, kicked the back door open, and turned to look at me. ''You gonna stay?''

His tone said it was a matter of indifference to him. He was leaving. I could accompany him or not.

"I'll stay," I said quietly.

I hadn't realized how tense I was till I saw his eyes flicker toward the curtains behind me. I reacted instinctively. The .38 was out of my purse, aimed toward the curtains, before I stopped to think that if someone were there it might be the cops I was waiting for. It wasn't. It was a dark-haired, dark-eyed woman who stood calmly in my sights, eyeing my revolver with regal indifference. Her hair was pulled back and tied under a bright cotton scarf. She wore a white cotton peasant blouse, heavily embroidered, and a floor-length, ruffled skirt that swirled gracefully with her every movement. A fringed shawl hung loose on her shoulders, ridiculous in the muggy heat of the little room. Her hands were out of sight, holding the curtain open.

I had no idea where she had come from. I hadn't heard anyone come in, but neither had she been in that candle-lit room when we'd passed through. But she was inarguably here now. "You go with him, *gadjo*," she said. "It is better this way." Her voice was soft, pleasant, her tone conversational. But I saw the look that passed between them. It was one of pure hatred.

This was an alien game, and I didn't know the rules. Nick did, and he wanted to run. But the first rule in my business is if you find yourself in the company of a dead body, it doesn't matter who killed him, you call the cops. Running only makes matters worse. I put the gun away. "Who are you?"

She smiled. It was not a nice smile. Her face was attractive in the same gaunt way Nick's was, but softer and more feminine. Her eyes were like black marbles. "I am one who has turned the tables, as the *gadje* say. Now it is my gun that covers you." She let the barrel show past the curtains. "Do as I say, whore. Run."

I could hear police sirens in the distance. I wondered whether she had called them, and what she planned to tell them if she had.

"If you do not go," she said, "I will shoot you now. I can say I caught you knifing that one—" she gestured toward the woman on the couch "—and defended myself. Then, perhaps, I will shoot my brother as well, who steals from his own family like a *gadjo*. That would give me great pleasure. It is his knife in that woman's breast."

There wasn't a lot of choice. I followed Nick out the back door, wildly trying to remember whether I'd touched anything inside. If I hadn't, maybe it couldn't be established that I'd ever been there. I was careful not to touch anything on the way out.

We passed through a dark, narrow corridor that reeked of stale urine and rancid cooking oil. Nick walked a little ahead of me, glancing back once or twice to make sure I was still with him. I stumbled over a bag of garbage and threaded my way past several more. Maybe once we were outside I could find a public telephone to call the cops. I didn't know any Oakland cops personally, but I did know we'd better report that dead woman and get our story in first.

We came to an outer door and Nick held it open for me. I went past him into blinding sunlight and a blast of oven-hot air. Behind us in the corridor I heard the ear-shattering report of the Gypsy woman's handgun. Nick lurched against me, pushing me out of the doorway, and kicked the door shut with his heel. "Run, jeez, run!" He grabbed my hand. "That crazy woman will come after us, now. Run!"

Something in his voice convinced me. None of this made a damn bit of sense, but I realized I could get myself killed, hanging around trying to figure it out. The lady certainly had shot at us. If Nick said she would keep it up, I believed him. It was as logical as anything else that had happened this afternoon.

I remember the sailboats' triangular sails dotting the bay and decided next time I caught someone trying to steal my car, I'd call the cops. If I couldn't be a member of the leisured class, at least I didn't have to be a damned fool.

We ran.

THREE

WE WERE IN a littered alleyway between rows of
two-story stucco buildings. The white concrete
pavement and the pale gray walls reflected the sun
in tangible waves of bright heat, which ripened the
ample contents of the many battered and lidless
garbage cans that lined the backs of the buildings.
It was like running through a sauna full of last
week's leftover dinners.

If I still had any questions as to the advisability
of running, Nick's sister cleared them up for me.
She reached the back door before we were halfway
down the alley, and the rest of the way our flight
was punctuated by the crashing report of her handgun, magnified between the building walls, and the
occasional splat of a misplaced bullet chipping concrete. It sounded like a small gun, maybe a .22.
With something that size she would be lucky to hit
us and not likely to do much damage if she did.
Still, I've a healthy respect for my gun. The human
body is an essentially fragile vessel, and it doesn't
take well to being punctured. It tends to leak. I
don't like situations where that becomes a possibility.

By the time we reached the end of the alley I was leading Nick. He had taken my hand to drag me away from the building; now I was half dragging him. Part of that was due to my reluctance to get punctured, but only part. At the time, I didn't understand why he had become increasingly slow and clumsy ever since he had lurched against me on our way out of the *ofisa* building. Later, when I did understand, I felt guilty for the way I had propelled him by main force through that rubbish-strewn alley, but at the time all I was thinking of was getting out of range of his sister's handgun.

When we emerged onto the cracked and weedy sidewalk I had the presence of mind to stop running. By the simple expedient of letting him run into me, I got Nick slowed to a reasonable pace, as well. It wasn't the kind of neighborhood in which the sound of gunshots attracted much overt curiosity, but if anyone *were* looking, he'd pay less attention to a passing couple who walked rather than ran. And unless someone actually saw us coming out of the alley, there was no reason to think we had anything to do with anyone in it.

Nick recovered from bumping into me and tugged at me to run again. "Come on," he said urgently.

I tugged right back. "I will, but slowly." So far, we had drawn only casual glances from the denizens of nearby rickety stairways and fire-escape landings. I wanted to maintain our low profile. "The car's just around the corner. And she's not going to follow us out into the street, is she? So there's no reason to call attention to ourselves."

"Oh. Right. Sure." He became aware of holding my hand and dropped it abruptly, looking confused. "Sorry."

"For what? Holding my hand? Or slow thinking?"

He glanced at me. His face seemed pale under the tan. "Both, I guess."

"Neither is a punishable offense."

"What?"

I grinned at him. "You're forgiven."

He was not amused. "You talk funny."

We continued in silence for a moment before I said, "I s'pose you need another ride."

That brought the wild look back into his eyes. "I gotta get outta here." For a moment I thought he was going to break into a run again. "She'll come after me. Or she'll send my father."

"Relax. I'll give you a ride for chrissake." We were walking fast, but not as fast as he wanted to. Still, he managed to restrain himself, to keep pace with me.

"Oh. Okay." He hesitated. "Why?"

"Why what?"

"After all this, why would you still, you know, why not just leave me?"

We had almost reached the car, and I was digging in my purse for the rotor arm. "You don't sound so much like a Gypsy now. I'd expect a Gypsy to take what he could get, no questions asked." I didn't tell the truth because I wasn't sure how he would take it. Nobody ever questions a man's desire to rescue a damsel in distress, but it's usually best not to discuss a reversal of roles.

"What do *you* know?" Something in his voice made me glance at him, but his face was a blank mask. Only the eyes were alive, and they were full of ghosts or questions I didn't understand. "Besides," he said, "I thought you didn't believe me, that I'm a Gypsy."

"After that experience, I'd believe anything. That was quite a charming little family reunion. Do Gypsies spend a lot of time trying to kill their relatives?"

"Usually not."

"Then what was that all about?"

"I don't know." He sounded genuinely confused. I didn't push it. While I replaced the rotor arm, he climbed docilely into the passenger seat and even fastened his seat belt without being asked. When I got in he was silent, huddled against the door, watching me with a look of mixed fear and defiance. There was something about him that reminded me again of small boys and puppies: something vulnerable and ridiculously fierce.

Neither of us said anything till I'd driven far enough south to catch the Grove-Shafter Freeway back to Berkeley. Then it occurred to me that I didn't know where he wanted to go. I started to ask, but when I glanced at him he appeared to have fallen asleep. His eyes were closed, his head relaxed against the headrest, his mouth a little open.

I smiled to myself and took the freeway to Berkeley. At the first gas station after we got off the freeway I stopped to call my partner, but she didn't answer either at home or at the office. She'd been on stakeout today. Probably by now she was in her boyfriend's cool, chlorinated swimming pool and didn't want to talk about work till next week sometime. It'd been a lousy day for anything, but probably worst of all for stakeout, sitting in a broiling car all day waiting for nothing to happen. I didn't call her boyfriend's house. She would not have thanked me for dragging her out of the pool to tell her I'd got myself shot at over something that wasn't even going to increase our income.

I didn't call the police, either. By then, it no longer seemed like such a good idea. If the Gypsies hadn't implicated Nick or me, there was no reason for me to do so. And if they had, it was already too late to get our version in first. I decided to wait and see what happened. Maybe I'd get lucky and nothing would. I'd learned my lesson already. Next time I caught somebody stealing my car, I'd call the cops. It would be much more pleasant to report an attempted theft to them than it would be to explain my way out of a Gypsy murder done in the wilds of Oakland.

When I got back to the Capri I found Nick awake and fumbling with the door handle. I'd had enough adventure for one day, but compulsive curiosity made me ask where he was going.

"I don't know. But you've done enough for me. For what you did, giving me a ride and everything, for that I'm grateful. Maybe my sister, she won't give you no more trouble if you're not with me." He got the door open and started to get out.

"I sincerely hope she won't," I said, watching him. "You know, you'll have to unfasten the seat belt if you want to go very far."

He looked at me in utter confusion. Then the words got through and he looked down at the seat belt. "Oh, right." He started to reach for it with his right hand, since the buckle was on his right, but his right arm didn't seem to work very well. He kept trying for a moment, frowned, and finally used his left hand to release the belt.

I thought it was the blow to his head. Maybe he had a concussion or something. "Nick, wait a minute."

He paused obediently, one foot out of the car, and looked back at me. His eyes were strange. "Yeah?"

"Listen, are you all right?"

It took a moment to register. Then he nodded. "Oh. Yeah. I'm, uh, you know, just…" He stared at me, frowned, and remembered that he had been speaking. "Oh, um. I better go."

"Nick, I think you need a doctor." It was a simple suggestion. I didn't mind driving the lummox to a doctor before saying good-bye. I wasn't ready for his reaction; it was stark terror. He half-shouted a denial and scrambled so frantically to get out of the car that I decided the lump on his head was his problem, what the hell. Then he turned, and I got a good look at his back, and leaned across the car to stop him. "No, you don't," I said.

The back of his beautifully tailored suit was dark with blood. One of his sister's wild shots hadn't been so wild: there was a neat little round hole in the shoulder of his jacket where the bullet had gone in. A lump on the head is one thing. Bullet holes are another. I wasn't ready to leave him bleeding all over the streets of Berkeley. "Why didn't you tell me?" I got him back in the car, enough so I could look at his face. It was set and pale.

"You didn't ask." He frowned in fierce concentration. "I won't go to no doctor."

I tugged at him, trying to get him all the way back in. "I know that, you dolt. Oh, for chrissake, get in! I won't take you to a doctor. You should've told me she shot you!"

"What could you do, put a Band-Aid on it?"

"Something like that. C'mon, I'll take you home."

"I got no home."

"I mean my home, lummox."

"I'm all right."

"Gypsies!" I was trying for the same tone he used when he was ready to leave me in the *ofisa*, before his sister showed up. I started the car, watching him steadily. "You gonna come with me?" It was hard to make it sound like a matter of indifference. Ridiculous as it seems, I was becoming fond of this macho lout.

He looked at me for a long moment while I held my breath, wondering whether I'd got the tone right; whether he'd recognize the connection; whether he'd remember the way he felt in the *ofisa;* whether it would make any difference if he did...

Then suddenly, blindingly, like sunlight after morning fog, he smiled. "I'll come." He got back in and with some difficulty got the door closed behind him. I helped him fasten the seat belt; his right arm seemed almost nonfunctional.

"That's better," I said.

"It's no big deal. It was a little gun."

"I know that." I pulled out of the gas station, headed home. "And I know better than to take a bullet wound to a doctor. Unless you're willing to explain the circumstances, which I think we're not.

But it still is a bullet wound, and you're in shock. You need treatment.''

He started to shrug, thought better of it, and frowned at me instead. "I still don't know why.''

"Why what?''

"Why you're doing this.''

"D'you have to?''

"Have to what?''

"Know why?''

He thought about it. "But what you're doing, what do you get out of it? What'm I to you?''

"I'm not sure. I suppose we could try on the word 'friend' and see if it fits. I can't think why else I'd let you bleed all over my upholstery.''

He grinned uncertainly. "You don't know nothing about me—''

"More than I care to, maybe.''

"—and you don't like what you do know. So how can we be, what you said, friends?''

"I don't know. We'll see how it goes. If it doesn't work out, we'll still have all the options open to us. I can get you busted for trying to steal my car. You can frame me for murder. We could form a suicide pact. Hell, we could even get married.''

"I don't understand you.''

"I know.'' I glanced at his worried face and relented. "Don't fret. I'm essentially harmless. You might even learn to like me.''

We made it home safely. "Home" was a two bedroom cottage on a corner in El Cerrito, two blocks from the BART station. That was for my husband's benefit, when I had a husband. He didn't care about the plumbing, the number of windows or kitchen cupboards, the color of the carpet—he didn't even care about the garden space in back. All he cared about was whether it was near public transportation and whether I would quit my job to keep it neat for him.

I did, too, for a while. Long enough to have a baby and find out my husband didn't have any idea who he'd married. In that order, alas, or I would've skipped having the baby. I stuck with him for a while, trying to make it right, but I couldn't take it. I suppose I had made promises I couldn't keep. When I put the kid in nursery school and asked my partner whether she wanted a partner again, my husband filed for divorce.

I got the house, he got the kid. That was fair enough. I wasn't a good mother. He wasn't a good housekeeper. Besides, he remarried straight away. To give our daughter a "normal home environment," he said. Which I couldn't offer either of them.

It's funny, though. I thought he knew what I was when he married me. He knew what I did for a living. I guess he thought if he married me, I'd automatically change my ways, grow up, settle down, and act like his idea of a proper woman. I did say I was willing to give it a try. I quit my job, joined the PTA, cooked dinners for his business associates and their wives, and drank too many gin collinses during the insipid, obligatory conversations that always went with the dinners. Well, hell. I hate cooking. The whole idea was just plain stupid, that's all. I'm not the happy-homemaker type. We both should have known that. But neither of us figured it out in time.

Nick looked surprised when I parked on the street beside my house. It was a nice little neighborhood but not particularly surprising, as far as I could see. The houses were all one or two stories, mostly white with chintz curtains or venetian blinds—very subdued, very demure, very proper. My neighbors were mostly old people who kept their lawns in perfect condition and rising young executives who hired Japanese gardeners to keep theirs even better. Mine was scraggly, but it was all right. The neighbors didn't like it, but that was their problem.

"You live around here?" Nick looked all around, as though in search of a likely dwelling.

I wondered what sort of dwelling he would consider likely. A twenty-story condominium? An Oakland tenement? An Indian tepee? "Right here." I pointed at the side of my little white house on the corner. "That one's mine."

He stared. "You *own* it?"

"Pay taxes and everything."

"Jeez. I never knew anybody who owned a house before. I mean…"

"I know what you mean. It's okay. Today is a day for surprises. I never knew a Gypsy before. Let's get you inside. Think you can make it?"

"Sure." He didn't sound sure, but he sounded determined, so I let him fumble with the seat belt and the door handle by himself.

For once I didn't bother with the rotor arm. I locked the steering wheel and let it go at that. By the time Nick was out of the car I was around on his side, the curb side, in time to catch his arm when he wavered. He put one hand on the car for balance and looked up the short slope to the sidewalk, glanced at me, set his jaw, and walked. When I saw he was determined to do it on his own, and maybe even could, I went ahead to unlock the back door before he got there. He wasn't going to have the strength left to pause for obstacles like locked doors. Forced to wait while I opened it, he just might collapse, right there in front of God and all my neighbors.

I paused at the gate to wave at Mrs. Brown's house across the street. She wasn't visible at any of the windows, but she never missed much. Nick's suit was dark enough that from across the street the spreading stain on the back might not be visible, and his unsteadiness might be attributed to alcohol, though Mrs. Brown was sure to suspect drugs. At least she couldn't see his face. It was so pale, so set with a peculiar look of inner-directed concentration, I felt like crying. It took a hell of a lot of courage for him to make it all the way to the door without help. He was in shock, which probably kept the wound from hurting him much, but left him dizzy and confused; but he made it.

"So you're a hero." I let him into my sunny yellow kitchen. "Now sit down. You've proved your point. I'll help you take off your jacket."

"What for?"

"So I can see how badly you're hurt."

"I told you, it's no big deal."

"I'd like to see for myself."

"No."

He started to get up, but I pushed him back. "Look, I don't know what your problem is, and if you don't explain it I don't see how I can find out. I want you to take off your shirt and jacket, so I can take care of the hole in your shoulder. Or call somebody who can, if it's more than I can handle, which it probably is. I think there's still a bullet in there. That can't be too healthy. So what's the big deal? What've you got to hide? You think the sight of your naked chest will drive me wild with lust and I'll ravish you on the spot or something?" I get silly at all the most inappropriate moments.

"No." He sighed heavily and tugged at the jacket. "I'll take it off." To my utter amazement, he blushed. "Just, I just, well…oh, hell."

"What is it?"

"Nothin'."

"You want to lie down? I'll let you bleed all over my couch, if you want to." I thought it might make him smile. It didn't. He looked at me as though I had taken leave of my senses and shook his head. "I'm okay."

I had to help him with the buttons on the shirt. He stood up to let me pull it off when we had it unbuttoned, then straddled a kitchen chair with his arms crossed on the back of it and his face hidden, his forehead resting on his arms. I put the shirt aside and walked around him to get at his shoulder. "There, see?" I said. "I'm not going to rape you on the spot. I won't even…" I lost my cool. In the process of getting the shirt and jacket off, I hadn't really looked at his back. All I'd seen was a lot of blood and the look in his eyes. Now I saw what he wanted to hide. "What the hell happened to you?" But I shouldn't have asked. I knew the answer.

His entire back was a tangled welter of thin, white scars. Most of them were old, though there were some more recent, still pink. There's only one thing that leaves scars like that. And the visible ones aren't the only scars it leaves.

"Nothin' happened." His voice was muffled against his arms.

"I know, Nick. I'm sorry."

He exploded. One moment he was sitting quietly, exhausted, on my kitchen chair. The next moment the chair was halfway across the kitchen and he was against the wall in the other direction, facing me, his eyes deadly. 'You don't know nothin'!'' He wanted to hit something. But this was my kitchen, and he contained his rage with a visible effort. "You don't know. You don't—oh, Jesus, jeez, don't *sound* like that, it's just my father, he don't—God *damn* it! I don't need your damned pity!"

I waited till I thought he was finished. "Nick."

"Gypsies, they *love* their kids. We don't, we aren't like you, but—it ain't—"

"Nick."

"Damn you." He said it without force of conviction.

It was like reaching for a wounded animal. He was confused, scared, hurt, and he wanted to hurt somebody back. If I wasn't careful, that somebody would be me. "Nick, I don't give a damn how Gypsies treat their kids. I don't care about your father, I don't care about your sister, I don't care about your whole damn Gypsy family. What I care about is you. And what I want to do about it is see if I can get that bullet out of your shoulder. That's all. I'm sorry I reacted badly. It's none of my business. I won't say anything more. So will you sit down, before you fall down? Please?''

"Why?" His anger was fading, but he was still sullen and unwilling to do anything I suggested.

"Because if you fall down, I don't think I can pick you up. And I don't want some damn Gypsy lummox lying all over my kitchen floor. Particularly not one who bleeds. Besides, right now you're bleeding on my curtains.''

He jumped away from the window as if it burned him, glanced back at the curtain, and saw I was lying. I shrugged and tried a feeble grin. He matched it, reluctantly. "Okay. Okay. Sorry."

"Sit down," I said.

He picked up the chair and sat on it. "What's a lummox?"

"A clumsy, stupid person."

"I ain't clumsy."

The doorbell rang before I could answer that one. I glanced out the front window, saw the cop car parked in front of the house, and restrained my panic. The spare bedroom was off the kitchen. I grabbed Nick's shirt and jacket and shoved him toward the bedroom. "Get out of sight and be quiet." The doorbell rang again. Cops are seldom patient.

"What is it?" He couldn't see out the front window from where he stood. Which was just as well, because it meant if there were cops on my doorstep, they hadn't been able to see Nick on their way past the front window.

"Just stay out of sight and I'll go see. Maybe nothing. Maybe a Fuller Brush salesman. Stay cool." I pushed him into the bedroom.

He looked doubtful, but he went. I closed the bedroom door behind him, glanced around the kitchen and didn't see anything out of place, and started toward the front door just as the bell rang again. From the living room I could see two cop cars parked in front. But the window and door were so arranged that I couldn't see who was on the porch.

Maybe a troop of seventeen uniformed officers, coming to take me away? "Oh, God," I said half-aloud. "She jokes. At a time like this."

I straightened the front of my dress, patted my limp hair as though that might do it some good, arranged my features in what I sincerely hoped was a polite, disinterested smile, and opened the door.

FOUR

THERE WERE ONLY two uniformed officers on my porch, not seventeen. My front door faced west and the late afternoon sun backlighted them so it was hard to see their faces, but with cops that doesn't really matter. I sometimes think they all wear the same grim expression, day and night. It reminds me of children chewing their tongues while they draw pictures. I wonder if cops look like that even in their sleep. But I've never got curious enough to find out.

"Miss Aileen Douglass?" asked one. There's something about the way cops ask that question. Like it was more accusation than inquiry.

"Yes." I felt as if I were admitting to murder. It didn't help that I'm short, and even standing one step down from me on the porch the two officers towered over me. I was used to being towered over, but sometimes I wasn't exactly pleased by it. This was one of those times.

"Police officers, ma'am," said the other officer. They were the same height and roughly the same weight. Their posture was identically military, their expressions identically solemn. Fortunately one

was blond and the other dark; otherwise, I might
not have been able to tell them apart.

"I can see that, thank you. How can I help
you?"

"Were you acquainted with a gentleman by the
name of William MacMurray?" asked the blond.

"I am," I said, and caught the past tense, and
stared. *"What?"*

"I'm sorry, ma'am," said the dark one. "Mr.
MacMurray is currently deceased."

The ridiculous phraseology didn't even register.
He was apparently trying to be polite. Like Nick,
he had an accent that sounded like New Jersey to
me. In Nick's case it made me think of Bruce
Springsteen. In this cop's case I tended more to
think of greasy-haired, not very bright young men
named Vinnie. Maybe El Cerrito was hiring cops
from the Mafia these days. It hardly mattered. The
important part was not how he phrased the information that Mr. MacMurray was dead. The important part was that Mr. MacMurray was dead. Mr.
MacMurray was my client. My only client. "Shit,"
I said.

"I beg your pardon, ma'am?" That was the
blond. He shifted his feet and looked hot. It was a
hot day.

I glanced at their badges—they were El Cerrito
cops all right—and stepped back from the door.
"I'm sorry, officers, I'm not being very polite.

Won't you please come in? I'm afraid your news was a little shocking. Mr. MacMurray was my client. Might I ask how he—what happened?"

The blond preceded the dark one into my living room and both looked around almost nervously. It was a fairly ordinary living room, carpeted a rather awful dusty rose and furnished in Early American Thrift Shop, with lots of windows to let the sunlight in. I like sunlight.

I gestured toward the ancient gray couch that I had tried to make more attractive by tossing little dusty-rose-colored pillows all over it. The effort had been wasted. Nothing would make that couch more attractive. The dusty rose color, a concession to that repellent carpet, was a major mistake anyway. I don't like dusty roses. It would have been better to pretend the carpet didn't exist and select accent colors I liked. "Sit down," I said. "Could I get you a cup of coffee?"

"No, thanks," said the dark one. They both sat down, so the rejection was of coffee, not couch. That was reasonable, on a day like this, but I hadn't anything cold to offer except gin, which I didn't think they would accept. The way the dark one was looking at me, I thought he might even bust me for offering it. He was trying to find something to bust me for. Or maybe it was just that I had bad breath. This might be one of those situations the television commercials warn us about.

They looked less nervous once they were seated. From the couch they could see all the living room and kitchen as well as the front bedroom door. The back bedroom door was out of their sight behind the refrigerator, and I hoped Nick would stay safely behind that.

I selected a blond fake Danish chair facing the cops and waited, dropping the polite smile. It was wearing thin, anyway. Now we were all on the same level, and that relieved some of the tension. Not all of it, though. They were careful to avoid undue relaxation. The blond wasn't as determined to dislike me as the dark one, but both of them looked as if they'd rather be anywhere else. Probably they had expected a lady detective to be of more formidable bulk than I. I must have surprised them. But they couldn't afford to relax on that account; murder suspects come in all sizes.

"I'm Officer Ripple," said the blond, "and this is Officer Kelley. I wonder if you might answer a few questions, ma'am?"

"Certainly. I suppose you've already checked out my profession and looked up my license?"

Ripple smiled carefully. He'd have been cute if he hadn't been constipated. "They checked at headquarters, ma'am. You say Mr. MacMurray was your client?"

"Yes, he was. I wonder if you could tell me how he, well, died?"

"He was shot, ma'am." He watched me attentively. "Through the head. With a .38 caliber weapon."

I made a face. "You'll want mine, then. For ballistic tests. Right?"

"Yes, please, ma'am."

"Okay, I'll get it. I keep it in a safe in the bedroom." I don't know why I said that. Sometimes I really say stupid things to men, especially those in macho professions like policemen, for no apparent reason at all. Maybe it's a hang-up left over from those years of trying to be a proper housewife for my husband. Maybe I thought a proper housewife would keep her gun in a safe in the bedroom. Why would a proper housewife have a gun at all? "D'you mind waiting here?" I turned away so they wouldn't see me blush.

"That'll be fine, ma'am."

On second thought, maybe the reason I said something stupid to them was that they kept saying something stupid to me. It was all I could do not to mimic that officious "That'll be fine, ma'am." These two were going to drive me crazy in short order. I'd made the acquaintance of several El Cerrito cops; it's a good idea, in my line of work, to be on friendly terms with as many cops as you can. But these two I hadn't met before. Their loss, certainly not mine.

I picked up my purse and went to the front bedroom, pulling out my keys on the way. There really was a key-locked safe in the closet, installed by the previous owner. Stupid device, openable by any competent teenager with a bobby pin, but having said I kept my gun in there, I had to make a show of getting it from there instead of just pulling it out of my purse. Not a bad idea, really, to avoid the sort of conversation that would so likely ensue with those two if they knew I carried it, loaded, in my purse. They might be afraid I'd shoot somebody by accident while searching for a lipstick.

Or I might just be getting cynical, in my old age, about such men's attitudes toward women. I used the sound of opening the safe to cover the noise made when I flipped the cylinder and dumped the cartridges into my purse. I closed the cylinder with one hand and the safe with the other and returned to the living room with an empty revolver and a box of cartridges. "Here it is, officers. I usually don't keep it loaded, but here's a box of cartridges. D'you need them, too?" A woman's best defense is stupidity. "And may I have a receipt?"

Kelley asked to see the paperwork on the gun and looked it over with extraordinary attention to detail while Ripple wrote out a receipt and handed it to me. His handwriting was about as legible as the average doctor's.

"This really is shocking news about Mr.

MacMurray,'' I said. ''When did he—when was he shot?''

''We found him this afternoon, ma'am,'' said Kelley. It came out sounding more like, ''We fownim dissaffernoon,'' but it wouldn't be possible to really do his accent justice on paper, so I won't try. ''The coroner's report will give us more information, when it comes in. We found this in his car. Does it mean anything to you?'' He handed me one of my business cards. My home address was scrawled in pencil on the back. That explained why they were here.

''It's my business card. I don't recognize the handwriting on the back.''

''It's not Mr. MacMurray's handwriting?'' That was Ripple, looking alert.

''It could be. I don't really know.''

''Do you know why he might have wanted your home address?'' That was Kelley, looking suspicious.

''No. I can't imagine. Where did you find him, by the way? I thought he lived in San Jose.''

Ripple answered patiently: ''We found him three blocks from here, near the BART station, in his car.''

''No witnesses? Nobody heard the shot?'' It was becoming a real effort to remain polite to these two.

''Not that we are aware of at this time, ma'am.''

''Why did Mr. MacMurray hire you, Miss Douglass?'' asked Ripple.

"Oh, um," I said, and after only a moment's hesitation decided on the truth; it seemed harmless. "He hired us to track down his fiancée. They had a lover's quarrel, and she left him. He wanted us to find her for him."

"And did you find her for him?" asked Kelley, obviously expecting a negative response.

I gave it to him. "Not yet. Which is too bad, because he wanted to patch things up with her."

"Maybe he should've hired a bigger patch kit," said Ripple.

I grinned. The line had been irresistible, in view of our relative sizes. "You blew it. I fed you a straight line, and you bought it. You made a joke."

For an instant they both looked startled. Kelley thought about trying to brazen it out, but Ripple grinned and Kelley, watching him, gave a resigned little shrug and relaxed. But he still didn't smile.

"You're right, Miss Douglass," said Ripple. To my surprise, he looked almost human. The whole grim demeanor disappeared. "Sorry about the act. Sometimes it's useful."

"I understand."

"I'm sure you do," said Kelley. He was still openly hostile.

"Were you currently in contact with Mac-Murray?" Ripple asked.

"Constantly. He insisted on daily reports."

"Is that customary?"

"No. Most clients don't want to hear anything but the end results. But MacMurray was really stuffy about it. I guess he wanted to make sure we were earning our per diem."

"Sounds like you didn't much like him."

I shook my head. "I really didn't. But we needed the work."

"So you'd just take anything that came along," said Kelley.

"What's your problem? You don't like private investigators in general, or did I forget to use pit stop this morning?" I half expected him to ask what pit stop was, but he just looked prim and ignored the reference. Maybe he knew what I meant, or maybe he thought deodorant was something that shouldn't be discussed in mixed company.

"Whether I do or I don't like P.I.s," he said, "it ain't a proper job for a woman."

"I see. Tell me, what's your position on policewomen? They should maybe stick to writing parking tickets?"

"I think that subject's irrelevant," suggested Ripple.

Kelley and I glared at each other. "You're right," I said reluctantly. "Sorry. Look, I really don't think I can help you. I don't know much about MacMurray except that he wanted to find his fiancée, and he didn't want to spend a penny more on the effort than he had to." I thought about it.

"He didn't even sound really fond of her, but some people are like that. I didn't figure it was any of my business."

"He never said anything to indicate that he might be in any kind of danger?" asked Ripple. Now that he was less intent on looking like a cop, I was beginning to like him.

"No. Nothing."

"What about the fiancée? Can you tell us anything about her?"

"I can tell you she's probably still in the Bay Area. Maybe in Oakland. Her name's Nancy Thompson, but she's probably using an alias. We almost caught up with her once, in the Mission District, but she moved. Maybe over here, maybe to the Haight; we hadn't checked out all the leads yet. Looks like we won't."

"You have a photograph of her?"

"Sure. But surely you could get this information from MacMurray's relatives?"

"He has none, at least not in California." Ripple was a lot more informative than he needed to be. I wondered if that was an unconscious effort to balance his partner's attitude. "He came from Chicago, but there are no surviving relatives there, either."

I stared. "He said he'd lived in San Jose all his life. Why would he lie?"

"Curiouser and curiouser," said Ripple. Straight

out of *Alice in Wonderland*. "'Fraid I don't know the answer to that one, ma'am."

"The photograph of Nancy is in a file at my office," I said. "If you'd like, I could bring it by the police station tomorrow after work." It wasn't much use to us, anymore. Without a client, we had no reason to pursue the woman. And no way to pay the rent.

"That would be extremely helpful, Miss Douglass," said Ripple. "Thank you very much." They rose simultaneously, Tweedledum and Tweedledee. "We'll run the tests on your revolver, and you can probably pick it up tomorrow afternoon when you come by the station."

"Thank you." I walked with them to the door. "Sorry I couldn't be of more help."

"We'll be in touch," said Kelley.

"Thanks for the warning." I grinned at Ripple and closed the door behind them.

My first concern was for the Gypsy in my spare bedroom, but before I could get to him the phone rang. It had a long cord. I picked it up and went on through the kitchen, carrying it, to see how he was. "Douglass," I told the receiver.

"Aileen, it's me." My partner. And me with only bad news. "I found Nancy Thompson," she said.

"It's too late. We don't have a client."

"Yes, we do," she said.

I pushed open the bedroom door and looked inside. It was actually cool in there, swimming with leafy shadows from the vine-covered north window that let in plenty of light but no direct sun and very little heat. Nick was lying on the bed, face down, snoring gently. I closed the door. "William MacMurray is currently deceased, according to the cops who just left here," I said.

"I know that," said Sharon. "Nancy wants to hire us to find out who killed him. Plus she's offered to pay us what he owed. That's two days' fee we can't get any other way. And she'll pay our usual fee in advance, for the job she wants done. Which is one we ought to do anyway, Ailie. We can't just let people kill our clients out from under us."

"That sounds obscene."

"Do you have to do that?"

"Do what?"

"Play word games."

"Sometimes I can't help myself. Sorry. Look, Share, I don't like to look a gift horse in the mouth, but how did Nancy know MacMurray was dead? It hasn't been on the news, has it?"

"She didn't kill him, Ailie."

"How can you be so sure?"

"Wait and see. There's a little something about her that MacMurray didn't bother to tell us."

"I hate surprises."

"I told her we'd meet her in the office in half an hour."

"I can't. I've got something I've gotta take care of, first. D'you know Dr. Steve's phone number?"

She was good at phone numbers. She rattled it off and then paused. There was a moment of silence. "Are you all right? What d'you need Dr. Steve for?"

"What do we usually need him for?"

"What's happened? Ailie, for chrissake— I'll be right over—"

"You're jumping to conclusions again. It's not for me. It's for a friend. Okay?"

"Who? What friend?"

"Nobody you know."

"Who? Ailie, I'm warning you..."

"See what surprises feel like?"

Another pause, while she thought about that. "You mean you don't even need Dr. Steve?"

"I need him. For a friend. But that's all I'm going to tell you right now. Call up our new client and tell her it'll take an hour."

"I can't. She didn't leave a number."

I sighed. "Then meet her, and stall her till I get there. And get off the phone so I can call Dr. Steve."

"Okay, but you better tell me what this is about when you get to the office."

"It's personal."

"For personal business, you need Dr. Steve?"

"I'll tell you about it when I get to the office. Give me Dr. Steve's number again?" She gave it to me and I wrote it down, then hung up and turned to find Nick glaring at me from the bedroom door.

FIVE

HE HAD HIS shirt and jacket in one hand and the back door opened with the other before I caught him. "Now where are you going?" I asked.

He pulled away from me, but stayed in the doorway, trying awkwardly to get into his ruined shirt. It was not an easy task with only one functioning arm. "You're calling a doctor," he said.

"Oh, for chrissake. D'you know who was just here?"

He got one sleeve on, but couldn't manage the other. I didn't offer to help. "No."

"Two cops. Now, if I were going to let you get turned over to the police, it seems to me it would have been simpler to tell them about you while they were here than to call in a doctor who would call them back when he sees your shoulder."

He paused in his struggle with the shirt sleeve. "Then who...I heard you..." He scowled at me and renewed his efforts to get into his shirt.

"Dr. Steve's an old friend. He won't call the cops. So wouldja calm down?"

He got his arm in the second sleeve and shrugged the shirt on, grimacing when it hurt his shoulder.

The wound didn't seem to be bleeding anymore. I didn't know whether that was a good sign or a bad one.

"Well?" I said.

He made up his mind and closed the door. "Okay. I'll stay." He glanced down at the jacket in his hands and made a wry face. "This was a good suit. I just bought this suit."

"Okay if I call Dr. Steve now?"

"Sure. It don't matter." He grimaced again over the jacket, decided not to put it on, and sat down, watching me. I noticed again how dark and shadowed his eyes were, and how vulnerable the high cheekbones made his face. His hair was just long enough to touch his collar in back. In front it fell in tousled curls that almost reached his eyebrows. It gave him a dark, brooding look that was as unnerving as it was sexy. Or maybe it was unnerving because it was sexy. I decided that was not a productive line of thought, and turned my attention to the telephone.

Dr. Steve said he'd be right over. He lived just up the hill from me, less than a five minute drive. He didn't ask any questions; he seldom did. He was a good friend. Sharon and I had helped him out of a tight spot once a long time ago. He never forgot it. Some men resent being helped by women. Dr. Steve not only didn't resent it, he was so grateful it was almost embarrassing. But he turned out to be a good person to know. He was seldom too busy to do us a favor, and he was fascinated by our work. This wouldn't be the first time I'd asked him to do something at least marginally illegal. For us, he pretended laws didn't exist. He trusted us. In fact, he'd adopted us, and we couldn't've got rid of him if we'd wanted to. Fortunately, we didn't want to.

While we waited for him to arrive I fixed two tall gin collinses, with lots of ice, for Nick and me. It was beginning to cool off outside, even though it would be a couple of hours till the sun went down, but inside it was still muggy. And I'd been wanting a gin collins for hours. I sat at the table opposite Nick and sipped mine appreciatively. There is nothing like the cool, piney tang of gin on a hot summer day.

"Those cops," said Nick. "Were they looking for me?"

"No. It had to do with my work."

"You in trouble?"

"I doubt it."

He gulped half his drink and leaned back, toying with his glass, avoiding my eyes. His fingers bumped against one another unsteadily. He rubbed the back of one hand hard across his mouth and looked at me. "You said mostly you repossess cars. The cops, what would they care about that?" He wasn't interested in the answer; he just wanted to talk.

"They wouldn't," I said. "Sometimes the work gets more interesting. D'you have any plans for this evening?"

"Plans?"

Another alien concept, maybe. He wasn't giving me his full attention. I didn't know whether it was just reaction setting in, or he was nervous about something in particular. Whatever it was, he was doing his best to conceal it. "I have to go out for a while, is why I'm asking," I said. "You're welcome to stay here if you want. Or I'll drive you somewhere, after Dr. Steve takes care of your shoulder."

That got his attention. "You would leave me here when you're gone? That's crazy. What I could do, I could walk off with all your stuff."

"You could," I said. "I'll take the chance." Maybe that was stupid, since I really didn't know a damn thing about him, but I didn't think it was a problem. Nobody's a perfect judge of character, but I was innocent enough in those days to imagine that I couldn't be way wrong. I figured Nick would steal from me only if he really felt he had to have whatever he took or the profit from its sale. In which case, he was welcome to it. Once. Besides, there wasn't much of anything worth stealing; I don't place that much value on material things, so I don't have a lot of them."

Nick sighed. "Then I'll stay. Tomorrow I gotta go back to Oakland. I got to find my baby sister. But there's no sense messing with that tonight. I'd like to stay. Thanks."

"If the Gypsies really frame you for that murder, you shouldn't mess with it anytime. You should call a lawyer."

He looked suddenly weary. "Prob'ly they won't. Prob'ly what they figure, they'd figure they've scared me off, that I won't hassle them about Lela no more."

"They have to do something about that dead woman."

"My father, he could just dump her somewhere. The others would help him. What he did was bad, but putting somebody in jail is worse. The cops could never prove nothing, not if the Gypsies decided to stop them. Usually they wouldn't do nothing like that, it ain't our way, just dumping somebody dead like that, but with my father... Well, he could do it. And nobody would turn him in. Gypsies don't do so good in jail."

"You're saying they'd help him get away with murder? That they could do that? Successfully?"

"It wouldn't be the first time." He seemed perplexed by my amazement.

"This isn't exactly the picture I always had of

Gypsies. You know, they're supposed to steal everything in sight, but according to legend they're basically harmless, loveable knaves ready to burst into song at the first screech of a violin. Not casual murderers.''

"Gypsies don't steal everything in sight. And we ain't loveable what-you-saids, any more than *gadje* are. And most of us, we aren't murderers.'' The words were impatient, but his voice was just tired.

"But you make your family sound like the Mafia.''

"You don't understand.''

"Then enlighten me.''

"Do what?''

"Explain.'' I pressed the cold, damp side of my gin glass against my forehead. "Tell me how you're different from the Mafia.''

"What do you care?''

I should have seen that coming, but I didn't. Fortunately, I didn't have to answer it. I didn't know the answer. I cared because I was involved? That was bull; I could kick Nick out as soon as Dr. Steve had taken care of him, and I would almost certainly never see him or any other Gypsy again.

I cared because I hadn't known there were any Gypsies left, and it was strange to think of a large group of people whose social structure was essentially alien to that of my society, living right in our midst without our ever knowing it? Plausible, but I could always look it up in the library.

Maybe I cared just because Nick was an attractive man and I was a single woman and the combination turned me into a romantic idealist? I didn't like that one. Mainly because I was afraid it was true.

Dr. Steve opened the back gate just as I realized I didn't even want to look for an answer. Not now. Maybe tomorrow. If Nick were still around tomorrow. If not...well, then I wouldn't have to.

"I guess I don't care," I said. "It sounds sleazy. A family that sells its children, for chrissake. Here's Dr. Steve. Forget I asked." Nick glanced up, saw Dr. Steve outside, and froze, every muscle tense, ready to spring into action. "Relax," I said. "I told you he's a friend." I opened the back door. "Hi, Steve. Come on in."

Dr. Steve was a tall, balding man in his forties with a ready smile and pale blue eyes like ice. He always looked concerned or sympathetic, even when he was smiling. I never heard him laugh. "Hi, Ailie," he said. He met Nick's wary gaze and turned on the smile. "I'm Dr. Steve Eysenk. You must be my patient. Never mind telling me your name, if you don't want to. And stop looking so worried. I won't bite."

Nick didn't move a muscle. "I don't need no doctor."

Dr. Steve maintained the easy smile, holding Nick's gaze. "I know. I understand. But it'll make Ailie feel better, so let's just go ahead and get it over with, okay?"

Nick hesitated, then shrugged his good shoulder. "Okay."

Dr. Steve carried a blue canvas athletic bag instead of the traditional black leather doctor's bag. He put it down in a square of sunlight that was turning the pale wood of the table to molten gold and nodded his head at the windows. "Maybe you should pull the curtains, Ailie, in case any of the neighbors get curious. It's late enough in the day that that shouldn't draw much attention. And bring me a desk lamp or something. That'll cut off most of the light, and I'll need more than the overheads."

I did as I was told, glad he wasn't going to try to get Nick to lie down. I should have realized he'd know how to handle the situation. He always did. He was taking just the right tone with Nick. Just the right mixture of breezy professionalism and gentle amusement over my supposed anxiety. Maybe if Nick had been more alert, more aware of what was going on around him, he wouldn't have fallen for it. But he wasn't; that was the point.

When he had everything ready, Dr. Steve opened his bag and glanced at Nick, appraising his attitude.

"I could give you a local anesthetic. It would help, some, but it wouldn't—"

"No shots," said Nick. He was straddling his chair with his arms resting on the back so Dr. Steve could get at his shoulder. The lamp I'd set up illuminated half his face and left the other side in shadow. He looked like nothing so much as a handsome hoodlum-hero straight out of the movies.

"I didn't really think so," said Dr. Steve. He had his tools unrolled from their protective flannel and laid out in gleaming rows. "Okay. This is going to hurt. Try to hold still, okay?"

"Sure." Nick set his jaw and stared stoically at the table while Dr. Steve set to work. "About that, what you said before," Nick said, "about selling children."

I sat across from him and he lifted his eyes to meet mine. They were dark, bottomless pits. The light from the lamp went into them and disappeared somewhere in the unfathomable regions of his soul. "What about it?" I tried to sound indifferent. It was like watching a rabbit cornered in a cage.

"It ain't selling, exactly," he said. "The money, that's a girl's bride-price."

"Her what?"

"Her bride-price. You know?"

"No, I don't know. Tell me."

His face was turning pale, but his gaze didn't waver from mine, and he didn't so much as twitch under Steve's hands. "Us Gypsies, we don't marry whoever we want to, like *gadje*," he said. "Usually a boy's father, he buys the boy a wife when he's real young. They don't, you know, the boy and girl don't sleep together till later, but they're married. The wife, she works for the boy. That's how they decide the bride-price, by how good she is at making a living. Okay? Is that what you wanted to know?"

"And you call that marriage?"

"Sure we call it marriage. It's marriage."

"Well, how can they tell how good a girl will be at making a living? You said your sister's thirteen. How can a thirteen-year old make a living at anything?"

"Oh, jeez, leave me alone, will you?" He closed his eyes.

"Sure."

Dr. Steve, who had listened to all this in silence but with an expression of amazed curiosity, selected another tool from his bag. "I'm going to remove the bullet now," he told Nick. "It'll hurt, and afterward I still have to clean out whatever debris it carried in with it. You'll just have to hang on and try to hold still. You ready?"

"I'm ready," said Nick.

I wouldn't make a good nurse. This whole process made *my* shoulders ache. I felt sick. It's one thing to see people injured, either accidentally or in a fight: it's quite another to watch somebody hold still and let someone hurt him. I gulped the rest of my drink and waited.

After what seemed an interminable interval of probing, during which Nick sucked in his breath audibly but held as still as stone, Dr. Steve removed the bullet and dropped it on the papers he'd spread on the table. "There it is," he said, "but we're not done yet. You okay so far?"

"I'm okay," said Nick. He didn't look okay. "What you're doing, you go ahead. Get it over with." He saw my expression and managed a peculiar half-smile. "It's okay, Ailie," he said. "It ain't that bad."

That blew me away. *He* was comforting *me!* "Sure," I said. "You're a hero. I forgot."

"I ain't no damn hero."

"Maybe that was a joke."

He considered that, while Steve did horrible things to his shoulder. "About my sister," he said. His voice was strained, but steady. "Gypsies grow up fast, you know? Lela, she's a real good pickpocket already. She ain't as good at fortune-telling as Sonja, but she can do it. And she—"

"She's a good pickpocket?"

"Sure." There was something like amusement in his eyes, mixed with pain and a defiant pride. "Well, what's she supposed to do? She's a Gypsy. She don't know no better. What's she gonna do, she can't get a job as a secretary or nothing, she can't read or write, so what job's she gonna get that's legal?''

"Why can't she read or write?"

"Gypsies don't do that." He actually said it with a certain perverse satisfaction. "We don't let our kids mix with American kids. We don't send them to no *gadjo* schools or nothing."

"You mean *no* Gypsies can read or write?"

"Usually not." His voice caught and he closed his eyes, but he didn't twitch.

"I'm nearly finished," Dr. Steve said.

"It's okay," said Nick. He opened his eyes and stared at me, waiting for me to continue the conversation.

It took me a moment; I had to search my memory for the topic. "Are you illiterate?"

"Am I what?"

"Can you read and write?"

"Oh. Illiterate. Yeah, I'm that. Most Gypsies are. Those of us that still live the life. Some, like in Spain and some other places like that, they send their kids to *gadjo* schools and they stay in one place and they even maybe don't speak Romany. But here most of us still live the life. I ain't sayin' it's a good thing. Or a bad thing. That's just how it is."

"How can you live like that?"

"What do you mean? You live how you live.

What kind of question is that, anyway, how can I live like that? How can I live like what? You mean 'cause I can't read an' write? Is that all you do?''

"It's part of just about everything I do.''

"Excuse me, guys,'' said Dr. Steve. "I'm pretty much finished here.'' He put down his tools and wiped his bloody hands on a towel. "This was a small caliber bullet, and it wasn't in very deep. I think the wound will heal okay by itself, but I'd like you to take some antibiotics for the next few days. You really should have a shot now, but you'll live without it.'' He put an oversized Band-Aid on Nick's shoulder, turned off the desk lamp, and moved around the table to face both of us. "You can put your shirt back on now if you want to.''

"Let me find you a clean one,'' I said.

"Whatever,'' said Nick. Relieved of the need to endure Dr. Steve's ministrations, he had relaxed his guard and lost his equilibrium. His face went pasty white, and he began to tremble.

"Would you lie down now?'' I asked.

For a moment I thought he would refuse. Then he nodded, staring at me in confusion. "Okay.''

"This is a normal reaction, don't be frightened by it,'' Dr. Steve said gently. He helped me guide Nick into the spare bedroom and get him onto the bed.

"Will he be all right?'' I asked.

"He'll be fine,'' said Dr. Steve. "I'm going to

give him that shot now. I don't think he's in any condition to argue. Then I'd like to hang around for a little while, just to keep an eye on his reaction. The blood loss wasn't dangerous, but he will need bed rest. Can you keep him quiet for a few days?''

''I doubt it.''

He prepared the antibiotic shot and administered it. Nick didn't even react. That scared me, but Dr. Steve reassured me and led me out of the bedroom. ''What was all that about selling children?''

''Why, d'you want some?'' I asked.

He grinned. ''No, I'm just curious.''

''It's Gypsy stuff. Nick's a Gypsy.''

''So I gather. I didn't realize there were still any Gypsies who followed the old Gypsy ways.''

''I didn't either. You want some gin? Or coffee?''

''Gin,'' said Steve. ''Thank you.'' He rinsed his hands at the sink, dried them, and took a seat at the table. ''Rots your liver, you know.''

''That's a very undoctorly thing to say.''

He grinned again. ''I know.'' He bundled up his tools while I fixed him a drink. ''Where'd you find this one?''

''This one what?''

''Stray.''

''Back to that again? I don't pick up strays all the time. D'you see any others around?''

''Just the one, at the moment.''

"Oh, hell."

"What?"

"Well, what're you, my shrink or something?"

"Or something." He zipped his bag shut. "I'm just curious. Where did you find him?"

"He was trying to steal my car."

"Oh, terrific. That's a great recommendation."

"He's a Gypsy, he don't know no better."

"If he knows enough to say that, he knows better."

I handed him his drink. "I know it. But he's all right, Steve. Really."

"Good-looking, too," said Steve, watching me.

I made a face at him. "Cool it, will you?"

"Just so you know what you're doing."

"When did I ever not?"

"You want an itemized list?"

"Oh, piffle. Listen, I gotta change clothes. I'm supposed to meet Sharon in the office about half an hour ago. Can I leave Nick in your care?"

"You're going to leave him alone in your house while you're gone?"

"Why, won't he be all right?"

His eyes glinted with amusement. "I was thinking of your belongings."

"Oh, that. We've already discussed that."

"You discussed it?"

"Sure. 'Scuse me. I'll be right back." I went to the bedroom, pulled off my backless dress, grabbed the first long-sleeved dress I saw, and put it on. I felt sticky and dirty from the long, hot day, but there wasn't time for a shower. I settled for fresh eye shadow and cheek gloss.

When I was ready to leave I glanced at my watch and picked up the phone to dial the office, to let Sharon know I was on my way. Her half an hour was well past, and she should have been in the office with Nancy Thompson by now. She would've called me if there'd been a change in plans. But although I let the phone ring a dozen times, there was no answer.

SIX

I LEFT NICK in Dr. Steve's care and hurried through long afternoon shadows to the office. Even breaking a few speed limits along the way it was a ten minute drive. I had plenty of time to think of all the things that could have gone wrong. I thought of a lot of things.

It didn't make sense to imagine that Nancy Thompson would have ambushed Sharon. But neither did other things that had been happening lately. For instance, the death of our client, William MacMurray. He was an innocuous dolt, overweight and underintelligent and just generally cheerfully stupid. Who would have reason to kill him?

Maybe dozens of people. I didn't really know much about him. But the answer I kept coming back to was Nancy Thompson. I had no logical reason for believing that. Just a gut feeling. Which was odd in itself because gut feelings of that nature were Sharon's department. And she was good at them. We'd solved several cases on the basis of Sharon's excellent, unfounded hunches. They led us to investigate areas we might otherwise never have questioned, and they led us to solutions that sometimes saved our lives.

But this time I was going jittery over gut feelings while Sharon was convinced that Nancy Thompson was okay, or at least that she hadn't killed her fiancé. What made Sharon so damn sure of that? And if she was right, then why weren't she and Nancy in the office right now?

I was more worried than I cared to admit. Sharon and I had been partners for a long time. Most P.I. work is dull, boring, and tedious, in that order. But when it does get interesting, things can happen pretty damn fast. If you're working with someone, you have to know you can trust her, absolutely, with no second thoughts.

I know a lot of people I'd trust to water my plants, or to make a bank deposit, or even to keep a secret. Of all the people I'd ever known, Sharon was the only one I'd trust with my life. It was reciprocal. And it was important. And I was scared.

I tried not to think about it. Unfortunately, what came to mind instead wasn't much better. Nick had been wearing some kind of spicy aftershave or cologne that reminded me of summer afternoons long past, and the way love and spring rain and forest shadows felt when I was a lovesick teenager. The scent lingered in my car. I was glad to get out in front of our office building.

The building was locked; the manager always

left at five o'clock and locked everything up behind him. The building was over a hundred years old, and looked it. The manager had told me that the owner was trying to get it registered as a historical landmark. I suppose that was a valid goal. Stepping inside was like stepping into a hundred years ago, only I imagined it had been quite an elegant place then. There were signs of that in the remaining marble tile and dark walnut paneling. But they were overwhelmed by cracked plaster, peeling wallpaper, and rusted radiators. The place was a wreck, which was why we could afford to rent an office there. But it was a beautiful wreck, and this afternoon it was swimming with dusty shadows cast by fading sunlight through the glass-paneled office doors: a silent, summery atmosphere in which my worries seemed almost silly. Almost.

The elevator was as old as the building. It was hand-operated, by a gentleman who went off duty about three-thirty or four o'clock every day (depending on his mood and the weather). Tenants and their clients who entered or left the building after that were obliged to use the wide wooden stairs. They creaked, and they had a distinctive odor like the dust-and-disinfectant of a grade-school building at the end of summer.

I went up in a hurry, taking the stairs two at a time. On the third floor I waited at the head of the stairs for a moment, listening, before I started around to our office.

The building was laid out in concentric squares. The corridor went all the way around, with offices on either side. Ours was one of the outside ones on the west side. On a clear day we got a beautiful view of the Bay.

I took the long way around, approaching our office from the east. It was less logical and therefore less expectable. But if I hoped to ambush a villain, I wasn't having much luck. From the northeast corner all the way down the north hall I could see our office door. There was no sign of anyone around, either inside or out.

The door had a frosted glass panel with our names painted in black: Atwood and Douglass, Private Investigators. The light from the setting sun came straight through the office to backlight the letters. If anyone had been moving around inside, I would have seen a silhouette on the glass. Nobody moved.

The last few feet of the north corridor I took very slowly, trying to keep one eye on our office and the other on the west corridor as it became visible. There was no one there.

Just as I reached our office I heard a door slam somewhere, and the sound of a woman's high-heeled shoes running. It took me a moment to identify the scrabbling noise that accompanied her as that made by a large dog, slipping and sliding on the smooth wooden floors. The acoustics were confusing; I couldn't tell where the woman was till I heard her start down the stairs. She must have been hiding in one of the offices I had passed in the south corridor. I ran for the stairwell, but by the time I got there she was out of sight on the floor below. I took the stairs two at a time again and managed to hit the second-floor landing just as the front door slammed behind her.

There wasn't much hope of catching her at that point, but I went on down on the off chance. I opened the front door onto an empty sidewalk. No pedestrians at all. I walked out far enough to look back, to see if she might be concealed in one of the neighboring doorways. No such luck. I cursed quietly and went back inside.

This time I didn't bother taking the long way around. The office door was unlocked. Inside was a scene of utter chaos. The filing cabinet was open, as were most of our desk drawers. The whole place looked as though someone had turned a few hungry chimpanzees loose and told them there were bananas hidden somewhere in the room. There were scattered papers, files, and paper clips; drawers had been dumped upside down on the floor; even the wastebasket had been upended, its contents spread liberally over the carpet.

All that I noticed at a glance and dismissed as

irrelevant. What caught my attention was the sight of my partner, sprawled in a careless tumble on the couch, her silky auburn hair forming a glowing halo around her pale, still face. I froze. My legs wouldn't work right. "Sharon?" My voice sounded funny. After a paralyzed instant I waded awkwardly through the debris toward her. "Sharon?"

She moved, and I started breathing again. She was only asleep. On the table near her limp out-flung hand were two coffee cups, both empty. Sharon's had traces of cream and sugar in the bottom, along with God knew what else. Obviously it was something with quite a kick. When I shook her, she started to snore. I dragged her to her feet and swatted her a couple of times. She opened her eyes, stared at me as if I were something so alien to her preconceived notions of the world that she couldn't even identify it, and suddenly smiled.

"Ailie," she said. "Hi."

"Hi, yourself." Relief made my voice harsh.

Her smile died abruptly. "I'm gonna be sick."

I propelled her hastily out of the office and down the corridor to the ladies' room. I'm small, but fortunately she's not much larger; otherwise, we'd've had a mess to clean up. As it was, we made it to the john just in time.

When she felt better we went back to the office. Neither of us said much. Sharon was still unsteady, but there was color in her cheeks and the vacant look was gone from her eyes. When she saw the mess in the office, she sat down on the end of the couch and said dully, "What a gullible ass I am."

"Probably. How d'you feel?"

She grimaced. "I'll live. Unfortunately." Ordinarily she was the prim and proper one. Just now she looked as though she'd never seen a mirror. Her hair, which had been fastened in one of her complex salon-style coiffures, was all over loose combs and bobby pins. Her mascara was streaked and her Prince-purple raw-silk shirt was rumpled. She yawned hugely and started pulling combs out of her hair.

Our office was small, but by dint of careful planning and a lot of arguing we had managed to fit into its limited space two small gray metal desks; a once-white filing cabinet, four-drawer letter size; a couch with faded chartreuse upholstery and scarred wooden arms, seating for three if they were friends; a Chinese blue Masonite coffee table in front of the couch; and a small wicker chair with a dirty rust-and-salmon striped corduroy cushion. Interior decoration courtesy of our local thrift shop. Usually the client sat on the couch and Sharon or I sat in the wicker chair. If we were both there, one of us sat at her desk or (if it was me) paced the remaining floor space. Sharon is better at sitting still than I am.

Now there was no floor space to pace. Every

surface was cluttered with the contents of our drawers and file cabinet. "What was this all about?" I asked.

Sharon yawned again. "I don't know." She tried absently to smooth the rumpled fabric of her shirt. It wasn't necessary. You could have dipped her in a mud puddle and she would have come out looking elegant. I never could decide whether it was her posture, her figure, or her attitude; maybe it was all three. Whatever it was, the net result was that she had class. In a Salvation Army store wardrobe she still managed to look like a million dollars. It helped that she was always able to find prizes like that raw-silk shirt, even at a Salvation Army store. "Can you tell if anything's missing?" she asked.

I had already checked her purse. Her keys, credit cards, and the miniature .22 that she referred to as a handgun were intact. Now I was rummaging through the odds and ends on the floor, stacking papers at random more by size than by subject, and gathering loose paper clips. Our typewriter, the only object of even dubious value in the office, was upside down, but it was there.

It occurred to me to check the files. I wasn't really surprised to find the MacMurray file missing. "The file on our latest so-called case is gone. It's not here, and I don't see it in this mess on the floor."

"Nancy probably took it," said Sharon. "She

seemed to think MacMurray left something with us. But what, d'you suppose?''

"I don't know. Did she say anything?"

"She might've said anything. I don't remember much after the first twenty minutes or so. I remember her talking to me later, but I don't remember what she said. Except she kept asking questions I didn't understand.'' She shook her head to see if any more pins would fall out of her hair. It was all down now, hanging in beautiful thick auburn curls all the way to her waist. I hated her for that. Both the color and the length. Maybe the curls, too. Mine was curly, but the curls were the kind that come out of a bottle and look like a singed haystack.

Sharon yawned again and looked around miserably. "I'm sorry, Ailie."

"Oh, hell." I kicked a wad of paper from the wastebasket. "Let's go home."

"I'm for that."

"We can figure this out tomorrow." I collected both our purses and headed for the door.

"Next week," said Sharon. "I'm gonna sleep till then."

"Fine. Next week." I'd have to call the cops in the morning, but only so they could verify to the El Cerrito cops that the office had been looted. I didn't know how the El Cerrito cops would react to the loss of the file. As far as I knew, there was nothing of much interest in it besides the photo of

Nancy, which they could probably get elsewhere. But the fact that Nancy took it made me wonder whether I'd missed something.

I didn't intend to tell the cops what had happened to Sharon. I'd make up a plausible story as to how the unidentified burglar got into our office. We would deal with Nancy Thompson ourselves as soon as Sharon was up to it. That was a personal matter.

Sharon waited while I locked the office, then wandered aimlessly down the hall beside me.

"What'd you talk about for the first twenty minutes?" I asked her.

"What?"

"You and Nancy Thompson. What'd you talk about? Before you fell asleep?"

"Oh." We were at the head of the stairs and she took my arm for balance and support. "Um, mostly about, um, her guide dog."

"Her what?" I remembered hearing a dog. A *guide* dog?

"She claimed to be blind. She had a guide dog and everything." She sounded defensive.

"That's why you thought she couldn't've murdered MacMurray."

"That's why."

"But, my God, if she were blind, he'd have told us."

"I know that. Now. And of course she isn't, I

remember that much. I remember her laughing at me. God, what a gullible ass I am. I actually felt sorry for the bitch.''

''Everybody makes mistakes.''

She yawned and stumbled. I caught her and we paused till she had her balance again. ''Sure. Everybody makes mistakes.'' She laughed suddenly, a bitter, harsh sound. ''But not like mine. I win first prize for incredible stupidity above and beyond the call of duty.''

We were all the way downstairs and getting into the car before she said something that made me begin to doubt that, on the grounds that maybe that prize was mine. I'd just opened the door for her, and she paused with one hand on top of the car to yawn. All the yawning was making her eyes water, and she wiped them with the back of her hand and looked at me, blinking owlishly. On her, even that looked good.

''Gypsies,'' she said.

''What?''

''Gypsies. Did you know there are still Gypsies?'' She turned and sat in the car abruptly, giggled, and pulled her feet inside after her.

I shut the door and walked slowly around to the driver's side, got into the car, and closed the door carefully. ''What about Gypsies?'' My voice sounded strange. I cleared my throat but had trouble swallowing. I started the car and looked at

Sharon. She appeared to be asleep. I reached across to shake her. "Sharon!"

"Mmmph." She opened her eyes.

"Sharon, you said something about Gypsies. Why?"

"Oh, I don't know. Um." She yawned again. If she kept that up, she was going to get a cramp or something. "Oh, I remember. Nancy said something about Gypsies. But I don't remember what, Ailie, are you mad at me?"

I realized I was scowling and looked away. "No." I pulled the car out of the parking place and started toward Sharon's apartment building. "I'm sorry. I didn't mean to seem angry." Maybe I was jumping to conclusions. Not everything to do with Gypsies had to involve Nick. But there was an awful sinking feeling in the pit of my stomach, because I knew this did involve Nick. God, I had made it so easy for him!"

"I'm tired," said Sharon.

"I know."

"She put something in my coffee." She sounded surprised.

"I know."

"I wonder why she did that?" She asked it in the voice of a small child wrongfully scolded, thought about it for a moment, and said with evident satisfaction, "Oh, I remember. She wanted to find something. Oh, and, Ailie?"

"Yeah?"

"She said somebody was going to search your house, too. Because MacMurray has your address, I think. So you should be careful, in case somebody tries to break in."

That settled it. I wasn't jumping to conclusions. "I'm afraid it's too late to be careful." My voice sounded flat and harsh.

"Why?"

"Because he's already there." I wanted to hit something. Or someone. I'd fallen for the whole damn thing. I wondered whether he had found it amusing. *"Damn!"*

"Shouldn't we stop him?" asked Sharon, wide-eyed. I'd never seen her like this before. It was like dealing with a rather stupid child.

"You're in no condition to stop anybody. Besides, MacMurray didn't leave anything with us, so what can he find?"

"Oh, right." She giggled again. I was suddenly grateful she wasn't into drugs or even drinking very much; this kind of behavior was already getting on my nerves.

I took her home. She lived in an ancient apartment building full of little old ladies, most of whom opened their doors a crack to watch us traverse the thinly carpeted hallways. I found it unnerving, but Sharon insisted they were all sweet old things. They baked cookies for her and borrowed cups of sugar from her and probably spent most of the rest of their time gossiping about her. She loved them.

Right now she was still too drugged to notice them or much of anything else around her. Once I got her to bed she really might sleep for a week. Certainly she would be out for the night. Tomorrow she probably wouldn't even remember how she got home. I tucked her in, got her spare handgun from her bureau drawer and put it in my purse, muttered to myself because it was another damned .22 instead of a nice sturdy .38 or even a .45, and turned to leave.

"Ailie." Her eyes were open, but just barely. "Thanks."

"You're welcome, partner." I managed what I hoped was an encouraging smile, but I didn't feel encouraging. I felt sick.

"What're you gonna do now?"

"What makes you think I'm going to do something, especially?"

"You have that look, you know, your mousehole look."

Once when I was getting particularly caught up in a case she said I looked like a cat in front of an occupied mousehole. Ever since then, she referred to that as my "mousehole look." I don't know what it looked like. Just then the main thing I was feeling was grim. "I'm going to find a Gypsy," I said.

SEVEN

ANY DOUBTS I might still have cherished died when I got home from Sharon's, looking for Nick. Nobody's a perfect judge of character, I'd said. Well, at least I was right about that. I wasn't a perfect judge of character. When he was through with it, my house looked a lot like the office. He'd conducted his search more neatly, but he'd been startlingly thorough. There was, naturally, no sign of him in residence beyond the lingering hint of that same cologne or aftershave that had bothered me so much in the car. He must have searched the place as soon as Dr. Steve left, then departed when he failed to find whatever he was after.

It was now nine o'clock, and getting dark outside. On impulse I called Steve to see what time he'd gone. Around eight, he thought. That left Nick an hour or less in which he had managed to go through every drawer, cupboard, shelf, and closet in my house. He'd pried open the safe in the bedroom. He'd dug through the clothes in my bureau and dumped books off my shelves. He'd even searched the refrigerator and the medicine cupboard. He hadn't left things strewn all over the floor the way Nancy Thompson had done at the office, but everything was disarranged just enough that I could tell what he'd done.

I kept a wad of spare cash in a hollow towel rack in the bathroom, a few hundred dollars for emergencies. It was not the best of all possible places to conceal money, but it was marginally better than the silly safe. When I saw that the fitting had been recently tampered with, I knew it hadn't been good enough to fool Nick, and I almost didn't bother to look inside. It seemed a foregone conclusion that the money would be gone.

It wasn't. He had taken it out, refolded it, and put it back, all of it. That bothered me, because it didn't make sense.

Well, I had said he wouldn't steal from me. But that was when I was still under the impression that our meeting and all that followed it was accidental. By now it had finally occurred to me that I used the same parking lot nearly every day, so it was not inconceivable that Nick could have known whose car he was trying to steal, and that he wouldn't be able to start it. It was an audacious way to find out where I lived and to get inside my house, but Nick was good at audacious.

He could hardly have foreseen that I would docilely go along with him all the way to Oakland and back, though. Or that he would be shot, which was what had finally led me to take him home with me.

Maybe it was a coincidence that he chose my car of all those in the parking lot. A small but persistent voice in the back of my mind argued that coincidences do happen. I ignored it. He had selected my car because it was my car, and okay, he hadn't known he would get shot, but he must have known he could get me to take him home with me one way or another. I felt as though I had been used, and I did not like the feeling. The fact that he hadn't stolen my money didn't make one hell of a lot of difference. It was a thoughtful gesture, but it damn well wasn't enough.

I put the towel rack back together and fastened it to the wall, then got Sharon's handgun out of my purse to check it out. It was a cute little nickel-plated automatic that fit neatly in a small purse or in a leg holster under a dress, and that was about the only point in its favor. It was inaccurate and unreliable, but it was better than no gun at all. I stuck it back in my purse and went outside to the car, got in, and started driving. I was on the freeway before I realized where I was headed, and why. I was on my way back to Oakland, because a man who had pretended to like me didn't; because someone I considered a prospective friend wasn't.

Realizing my motives were impure didn't even make me slow down. So I was pissed, so my vanity was involved. So what? There are worse motives for doing things. Also, I had a score to settle with

Nancy Thompson, and she was involved in this thing somehow. While Nick was ransacking my house, she was cheerfully drugging my partner into a stupor. It wasn't absolutely necessary that I wait till Sharon was recovered enough to bring the matter to Miss Thompson's attention, if I could do it sooner by myself.

I parked a block from the *ofisa* and entered the building by the back door. The lock was a simple spring-loaded affair a child could have picked with a lollipop stick. The police keep encouraging people to install deadbolts, and people keep ignoring them. I'm all for it; I can't pick a deadbolt.

From the street, the *ofisa* had looked dark and deserted. That didn't necessarily mean it was. I traversed the dark, littered corridor cautiously, and listened at the inner door for several moments before I tried the knob. There was no sign the police had been there; Nick's father must have dumped the murdered woman's body somewhere, as Nick had said he might. It was very quiet inside. The lock hadn't been fixed since Nick broke in. The knob turned easily. I edged the door open and the heavy scent of sandalwood incense wafted out to greet me. The room inside was black. Not a pinpoint of light showed from the street in front. Still no sounds. The room had an empty feeling. I took a chance and lit the miniature flashlight I carry in my purse.

There was no reaction to the sudden light. I made sure the heavy curtains that divided the two rooms of the *ofisa* were closed, then played the light around the back room to be sure it was empty before I slipped inside and shut the door behind me. Then I flipped off the flashlight and stood waiting in the oppressive darkness, listening for some reaction from the front room. There was none. Hands outstretched before me, I edged toward the dividing curtains and parted them just enough to peer through. Enough light filtered past the window curtains from the streetlights outside to show that the front room, too, was empty. Nobody home.

I let the curtain drop and flipped on my light again. The back room was not large. It took only a couple of minutes to give it as complete and untidy a search as Nancy had given the office. I was careful not to touch anything that would retain a fingerprint. I doubted they'd call the cops, and even if they did, nobody was going to make a wild run through all the fingerprint files to see if he could find a match. What the cops use fingerprints for is as evidence against a perpetrator who has already been caught. Still, I'm a great believer in caution in all the wrong places.

There was nothing of interest in the back room. I moved to the front room, where I had to be more circumspect because my flashlight might be seen from outside. The only furnishings there were a marble-topped table, loaded with candles, and two defeated-looking chairs. One was a wooden kitchen chair with the seat split front-to-back and mended with silver duct tape. The other was a hideous orange velvet overstuffed easy chair that could have used some mending. I checked the underside of the table and the wooden chair and lifted the cushion of the easy chair. Reaching down beside it I found two buttons, a quarter, and a maroon plastic cigarette lighter. I let the cushion drop, and knelt to reach underneath the chair.

A corner of the cheesecloth lining on the underside was loose. I tore it off, expecting great things, but nothing fell out. I felt around among the springs and found nothing but dust. Finally I gave up on the furniture, dusted my hands, and investigated all the walls behind the curtains. I didn't know what I was looking for, but it didn't matter; I didn't find anything at all. When I'd checked all the walls, I returned to the back room and looked around again. But there was still nothing of particular interest. This whole search was a futile, wasted effort. All I'd learned was that I really very much disliked sandalwood incense. For that I risked losing my license on a breaking and entering charge. You'd think I'd know better.

It was sheer luck that I happened to be looking at the doorknob when someone outside turned it. The shock nearly immobilized me, but I had the presence of mind to flip off my light and slide quietly into the front room, pressing my body hard against the side wall behind the cobwebby curtains. There wasn't time to get to the front door, and anyway I didn't know whether it could be unlocked from the inside. I held my breath and wondered rather wildly whether my feet were visible beneath the hem of the curtains, like the villain's in a grade B movie.

Someone stepped through the back door so quietly I probably wouldn't have heard him if I hadn't been listening because I had seen the knob turn. I inhaled a lungful of dust and cobwebs and waited, praying I wouldn't sneeze. Whoever had come in didn't seem to be any more anxious to be discovered here than I was. But he was more familiar with his surroundings. Without turning on the lights, he went directly through the center opening in the curtains between the two rooms. I slithered cautiously into the back room again, in case my shoes were showing. There was just enough room to do it without disturbing the curtains noticeably, though I certainly disturbed a lot of spider webs.

At that point the sensible thing would have been to come out from behind the curtains and make a dash for the back door. But I've never been noted for my good sense in a situation where I could, instead, satisfy my curiosity. I stayed behind the curtains and waited.

He went right to the overstuffed chair. I found a torn seam in the curtains through which I was able to see his silhouette against the windows as he bent over next to the chair and reached underneath. No hesitation, no random searching; he knew exactly what he was looking for and where he expected to find it. But there wasn't anything there. When he discovered the torn lining he paused, then abruptly upended the chair, though he could hardly have seen much in the half-dark of reflected light from outside. He held the chair balanced on two legs and used his free hand to search the whole underside, then let it drop with a thud. "Oh, jeez," he said aloud.

I had almost talked myself into leaving, but when I heard that voice, I froze. That was just as well, because before I could make up my mind what to do about the situation, the back door opened and yet another interloper crept in. Soon we could have a party.

This one was a woman, and she wasn't wearing crepe-soled shoes like mine. I could follow her progress across the room without seeing her. When she paused for a moment by the back door, I peeked into the front room to see what Nick was doing. His silhouette was still visible crouched next to the velvet chair, and I thought I saw the glint of his eyes in a stray shaft of light from the street.

The woman crossed the back room confidently,

her high heels clicking on the concrete floor, till she bumped into the edge of the couch and paused, cursing softly. She was almost far enough into the room that I could dodge out the door she had left open behind her, but I would have a better chance of leaving unnoticed if she joined Nick in the front room, so I waited, breathing cobwebs.

She stopped cursing and tilted her head, apparently listening. Neither Nick nor I moved a muscle. We made quite a little threesome, all listening to each other listen. After a moment the woman whispered softly, "Nickie?"

I hadn't thought he could get any quieter, but he did.

She spoke aloud, but still very softly. "Nickie, I know you're in here. Where are you?"

Very, very slowly, without making a sound, he edged toward the front door. She waited, listening, then moved carefully around the couch toward the curtains. My eyes had adjusted to the darkness well enough that I could just make out her shadowy form against the patterned curtains. She was carrying something in one hand. Something that caught a dull reflection of light from the other room. Something she held pointed out in front of her like a deadly, accusing finger.

There wasn't time to go for Sharon's little gun, buried somewhere in the bottom of my purse. Nick was not going to make it to the door before the woman fired. I didn't stop to think what I was doing, or what he had done. I saw again the look in his eyes when he talked about his little sister, and I dived—not out the door, which would have been sensible, but at the woman's legs, which wasn't. "Nick, run!" I shouted.

She tried to turn, to aim at me, but there wasn't time. The gun went off with an ear-shattering roar as she went down under my weight. It left me nearly deafened, but through the ringing in my ears I heard the front door open and slam closed behind Nick. He was safe. I wasn't.

The woman beneath me got a sturdy grip on my hair and yanked my head back, at the same time kicking my shins with the pointed toes of her hard leather shoes. I had no idea where the gun was. It seemed logical to assume that it was still in her free hand, the one that wasn't busy trying to pull my hair out by its roots, and that at any moment she would use it to kill me. I had lost my purse in my dive, so there was no hope of using Sharon's .22 against her. My shoes weren't as deadly pointed and hard-soled as hers, and anyway she managed somehow to dodge the most vicious of my kicks. Her hair was tucked safely under a scarf where I couldn't easily get at it even if that had occurred to me, which it didn't.

She was fighting like a woman. So I did a stupid thing: I fought like a man. I slugged her. It was simple, quick, and efficient—and it nearly broke my hand. But at least it put the woman out of commission for a while. I put my bruised knuckles in my mouth and scrambled crabwise across the floor, searching with my other hand for my purse. I found it, slung it over my shoulder, and considered the situation.

Somebody might report the gunshot, but unless there was a cop close by, I had a few minutes' grace before I had to be out of there. I went back to the woman, found her purse, and flipped on my flashlight to examine the contents. My right hand ached and was already beginning to swell at the knuckles. I ignored it.

The prize was Nancy Thompson herself. She was also Nick's sister Sonja, who had already tried to kill Nick once that day. When I saw her photo on a California driving license, I turned the light on her sleeping face. They matched. Now that I had time to study her in less stressful circumstances, I realized that a different hairstyle and the judicious application of makeup would make it match the photo of Nancy Thompson that MacMurray had given us. I should have seen that when we were in the *ofisa* before, but it wasn't hard to excuse myself on the grounds that I do get nervous in the presence of unexplained corpses and hostile handguns.

Now the missing MacMurray file made sense. If she were illiterate, as Nick had suggested, she might have recognized MacMurray's name and would certainly have recognized her own photo, and she probably stole the file on general principles, unable to tell what else it contained and uncertain whether there might be anything in it of value to her or anything that would help us trace her.

She had an impressive assortment of credit cards in her wallet, but nothing else of interest except a hotel key. I made a note of the hotel name and room number and replaced everything the way I had found it, careful to smudge all the smooth surfaces that might hold a print. I really get paranoid about fingerprints sometimes.

Then I checked the gun she had dropped when I tackled her. It was a .38 revolver. Perhaps the very one that had shot MacMurray. I didn't touch it. I decided to get out before the cops got there. If they arrived soon enough, Miss Thompson might have some interesting explaining to do. And if I called them from the nearest pay phone, just in case no one else had, that should assure their prompt arrival before she woke up. Too bad I couldn't hang around to hear her answers to some of the questions. But I wasn't anxious to answer any myself.

At least I had evened the score some. And if Miss Thompson did manage to evade the police, I knew where to find her.

I wiped off the doorknob on my way out, and

wended my way carefully around the heaps and bags of garbage that seemed to be a permanent fixture of this corridor. I didn't realize how awful the entire place smelled until I got outside and inhaled the sweet, pure smog of Oakland. I'll take smog any day over sandalwood incense mixed with garbage. Sure, the smog'll kill me quicker, but at least I'll be more comfortable while I die.

The alley was almost as black as the *ofisa* had been; there was only one street light, all the way at the end. I hadn't really noticed on my way in how quiet it was. I'd been too intent on my mission of anger. Now that was shot, too. I had intentionally saved Nick from Nancy's wrath, and by so doing had let him and therefore presumably all the other Gypsies know I'd been there. Which would convince them I knew more about this MacMurray business than I really did.

Well, so be it I was angry with Nick, but not enough to want to see somebody kill him. Now if only he'd return the favor should the occasion arise. I felt sure the occasion would arise. I just didn't realize how soon. I was barely out of the alley before they jumped me.

EIGHT

THERE WAS HARDLY any change in light as I stepped from the narrow enclosure of the alley onto the gloomy sidewalk between the still, squat forms of parked cars and the windowless ground-floor walls of buildings that still radiated the unaccustomed heat of the day. I was on my guard, starting at shadows, but I didn't see or hear any sign of danger till someone grabbed me by the shoulders from behind.

I didn't feel like playing games. I reached behind me and grabbed his crotch, hard. He released my shoulders with a strangled cry. I whirled to face him just as two others emerged from the black maw of an areaway near the end of the alley. The one who had stopped me was temporarily out of service, but the other two moved toward me in grim and deadly silence. They were all three larger than I by a considerable measure, and now that I'd shown I wasn't squeamish, they were cautious. I would not catch another of them off guard so easily.

Their silence was unnerving. Even the one I'd hurt made no sound beyond a few anguished curses in what I guessed was Romany. They looked like Gypsies. They had that same dark, wild-eyed look Nick had, but none of the vulnerability that made him so beautiful. Their faces might have been carved in stone; the jagged lines and planes were like cold, carved granite, too sharp and hard for flesh, and the glitter of their eyes was like polished marble, smooth and wet.

Whether they knew who I was, or whether this was just a random mugging on a whim I couldn't tell, but from their determined silence and the fact that nobody went for my purse, I guessed it was the former. That had to mean they had watched me go into the *ofisa,* and waited for me to come out. If they had watched me go in, had they also watched Nick and Nancy go in, one after the other, while I was still inside? If so, Nick might have found a welcoming committee outside the front door when he fled. I hoped not, unless he got a friendlier welcome than I did.

I didn't have much time to dwell on it. The two I hadn't hurt were angling for position on me, their hard faces unreadable, their lithe bodies poised in graceful fighters' stances. The only advantage I had was that they had no idea how well I could fight. They knew I was willing to play for keeps, but maybe they thought the first injury I'd caused was a lucky accident. It wasn't.

They rushed me together. The one I had hurt was

still out of commission, but he watched. His eyes were hungry. He wanted them to hurt me. Instant revenge.

The taller of them reached for my neck with both clawed hands, the muscles of his shoulders and arms bulging under the sweat-soaked fabric of his white cotton shirt, while the shorter one danced lightly around and behind me. I ducked the tall one's hands and turned, kicking viciously sideways with a rigidly stiffened leg, catching him in the balls: a dangerous maneuver for both of us, since if he had seen it coming he could have dodged my foot, grabbed it, and had me on the ground with one sharp jerk on my leg; but I was lucky. He didn't see it coming. The advantage of doing it that way was that it kept the shorter one in front of me. I clenched my hands together and brought them down hard on the bridge of his nose just as he reached for me. I think I broke it. He still reached for me, but he couldn't see straight. He missed.

Men shouldn't leave their delicate parts unprotected like that when they attack somebody. I guess when they fight among themselves they have certain unspoken rules as to what's "gentlemanly conduct" and what isn't. But I'm no gentleman. When somebody attacks me, I don't stand on ceremony; I do what I have to do and run like hell.

I ran. None of the three followed me. I'd been luckier than I deserved. I'd made some stupid moves, and three against one is terrible odds. By all rights I shouldn't have been able to take them all. But sometimes it's hard for men to understand that their opponent isn't a gentleman, even when that's exactly the reason they're attacking her. This had been one of those times. The combination of my unexpected viciousness and the speed with which the whole thing went down—and the lucky fact that each of my three blows connected on the first try—left my attackers virtually defenseless. But I knew if they had time to think about it, I wouldn't have a chance.

I didn't give them the time. Knowing I might have to leave in a hurry, I'd left the car unlocked and the rotor arm in. I jumped in, started the engine, and didn't slow down till I was several blocks away. By then, reaction was beginning to set in and I had to slow down to keep from hitting something. I was shaking all over.

That was close. I don't like it when things get that close. And I really don't like it when not only are things getting rough, but I don't know why they're getting rough.

I didn't even have a client. All I had were a lot of clues that led nowhere. Answers, but I hadn't asked the questions. I didn't know what questions to ask. I didn't know what problem I was trying to solve.

Staying alive would be a good place to start. It

appeared that my continued health and well-being might depend on my figuring out what was going on.

I remembered suddenly that I'd meant to call the cops and tell them where to find Nancy. Damn. Too late now. By the time I found a phone, she would be gone from the *ofisa*, if she wasn't already.

At least I had her hotel name and room number, so it was likely I could find her again. I didn't know whether I would give that to the police. I needed time to think about it. Of course, if they asked, I'd have to. But if they didn't ask?

Well, they weren't asking yet, so I didn't have to decide yet. I put the Capri in gear and headed back to Berkeley, to Sharon's apartment building. I wanted to make sure she was okay, and then I wanted to go home to bed. It was late, I was tired, and I ached in every bone and muscle. There was nothing more I could do tonight; or at least, if there was anything, I had no idea what it was.

Sharon's apartment building, when I reached it, was dark and silent, all the windows blankly reflecting the colored floodlights that shone all night on the ragged borders of bird of paradise and century plants surrounding little brown patches of dicondera that served as a lawn. All the little old ladies were safely in bed and, presumably, asleep. I had keys to the downstairs door and to Sharon's apartment, so I didn't bother ringing; she was probably asleep, too, and I didn't want to wake her. I let myself into the building and tramped wearily up the flights of dreary, dimly lighted stairs and down the dusty corridor to her apartment.

I didn't need the key to her door. It was already ajar. When I saw that, I'm afraid I lost my cool. I knew I should have stayed with her. I should have realized that when they didn't find what they wanted in the office or in my house, they would come here. But I left her drugged and alone, completely defenseless, and went off on a damn fool vendetta against a Gypsy who shouldn't mean a damn thing to me. A vendetta that got me no answers but a lot more questions, a set of badly bruised knuckles, and a terminal case of the jitters.

"God *damn* it." I pulled out the little .22 automatic, jacked a cartridge into the chamber, and kicked open the door. I went in low, flipping the light switch and ducking sideways in one smooth motion, hoping the element of surprise would give me at least a small edge over anyone inside.

The living room was in chaos. It looked like Nancy's work. She must have followed us here when I brought Sharon home, and torn the place apart while I was busy feeling sorry for myself over Nick's behavior at my house. There was no sign of her or of anyone else here now. No one reacted to my sudden entrance, not even Sharon.

That scared me. I'd let the door slam back

against the wall with a startling crash. Even if she were asleep I would have expected her to hear it.

The floor between the front door and the bedroom was littered with debris—books from her shelves, knickknacks from her table tops, papers and pictures and pencils and all the odds and ends from emptied drawers and ravaged cupboards—but I plowed my way through it all in good imitation of an irate bulldozer. I didn't much care, just then, what I might break in the process, including me. I wasn't really even aware of the obstacles in my path. I wanted to go to the bedroom. I went.

She was sprawled gracelessly across the bed in a welter of sheets and rumpled blankets, peacefully asleep and snoring just a little, smiling with the cherubic innocence of a child. She was still drugged; she probably would have slept through a bombing raid. The ransacking of her apartment and my subsequent noisy entrance were disturbances far too minor to have interrupted that sweet oblivion.

"Oh, God." My voice wavered. I stared at the wreckage around her, and at her gently contented smile, and I sat down abruptly on the nearest object to me. Fortunately it was a chair. My knees wouldn't support me any longer; I needed something that would.

Twice in one day was just too damn much.

I had been telling Sharon for months that her front door lock wasn't adequate. You could open it with a credit card. There's a law in Berkeley that landlords have to supply and install deadbolts. Sharon's landlord never seemed to get around to it. He damn well would, now.

As soon as I was able to stand up again, albeit unsteadily, I spent some time putting the bedroom back together. I didn't want her to wake up in the morning to the sight of that unholy mess. Then I left her a note to prepare her for the sight of the living room, taped it to the inside of the bedroom door, and left. It was very late, and I was very tired. Her lock, such as it was, would last her the rest of the night; there was no reason to believe the Gypsies would come back.

On the way to the car I began, perhaps inevitably, to think of Nick again. I had felt attracted to him, I had trusted him, and I knew I had been wrong in that. He had betrayed my trust and ransacked my cottage. I had been taken in by a charming hustler, whether I wanted to believe it or not. Nancy Thompson was certainly my enemy, though I did not understand her goals, and Nancy Thompson was Nick's sister. He was working with her. Yet I had seen her make two apparently determined efforts to kill him. Like everything else about this case, it made no sense.

The attempt she made that afternoon could have been intended only as an act to convince me Nick was on my side against the other Gypsies, and the bullet that hit him could have been a wild shot after all; those little guns are difficult to hit somebody at a distance, yes, but to miss him? That shouldn't be any problem. Moreover, this evening Nancy hadn't even known I was there when she tried to kill Nick.

Or had she known? The three guys waiting outside could have told her I was there. It *had* been rather extraordinary luck that I was able to overwhelm not only her but the three of them, and with relative ease. I'm good, but I'm not *that* good.

Yet surely it was all too elaborate to be a hoax. For what purpose would these people have mounted such a complex and bewildering hoax against us? For what purpose had Nick tricked me, and Nancy Thompson tricked my partner, and both of them searched our homes and our office? What had they been looking for? What could we possibly have that they wanted? Whatever it was, why didn't they simply ask for it and be done? If I had it, I might have given them it. I owned nothing in the world worth dying for. But then, I owned nothing in the world worth the trouble of this bewildering hoax, either, if hoax it was, and what else could it be?

I had a headache. I had badly bruised knuckles and an only slightly less bruised ego. I was confused, and weary, and I wanted to sleep.

But when I got home, Nick was waiting for me.

kill him.

NINE

I DIDN'T SEE him till I had climbed the grassy slope
and crossed the sidewalk to reach the gate. The
back porch was in deep shadow, screened from the
streetlights by the weedy hedge of pungent herbs I
had planted around it. He was sitting on the concrete step, his back against the door, a darker shape
in a pool of black. I froze with my hand on the
gate, paralyzed by an uprush of pure, primitive terror at sight of a nameless *something* blocking my
way. There had been too many terrors in this night.
I could not cope. For one heart-shaking moment I
could not translate that shapeless black into any
recognizable form; and when I did, when it re-
solved itself before my stunned gaze into a human
shape, I still could not beat down the gibbering horror that cascaded its alternate waves of flame and
ice through my veins and turned my knees to
rubber.

I don't know how long I stood there before I saw
the glitter of reflected light in his eyes and realized
he was watching me. At the same moment, I recognized him at last, and all the terror turned in an
instant to sheer rage. I wanted to kill him. Instead

I said, as evenly as I could, "Waiting for a chance to finish the job your friends started at the *ofisa?*" I didn't open the gate. Instead, I leaned against it. The anger had begun to dissipate. I was too tired to sustain it. Perhaps the really sensible thing at that point would have been to get back in the car and go get the cops, but I didn't do that, either.

He didn't move. "That money," he said. "Part of that's mine. I want it, and, you know, MacMurray, he's dead anyway. Give me my share of the money and I'll go. What you do with the rest of it, that's up to you." He had his knees drawn up, his arms extended across them, his hands dangling gracefully. The shirt he was wearing had once belonged to my husband. I kept it to wear when I was cleaning or painting or performing other untidy tasks. It looked better on Nick.

"If you wanted my money," I said, "why didn't you take it when you were here before?" It came out sounding as exasperated as I felt. "Can't you just steal, plain and simple? D'you have to go through this cloak-and-dagger routine?"

"What I want, it ain't stealing if I get it. Maybe before, when MacMurray had it, maybe then it would be stealing, but he don't need it no more. And what you might not understand, you know, is that *we* pulled the *hukkaben,* so why should you get the money?"

"*Hukkaben?*"

"That's a trick. A con."

"Oh." I opened the gate. He still didn't move. "Look, wouldja just get the hell off my back porch? I don't know what you're talking about, and if you want the truth, I don't want to know. I'm sick of the whole damn mess. So just go away, okay?"

"I ain't going no place." He grudgingly stood up to get out of my way when it became apparent that otherwise I might simply step on him. I think I would have, too. "I ain't leaving till you give me my money."

"I don't have your damn money." I unlocked the back door and let him follow me inside, don't ask me why. I could have insisted he leave before I even opened it, or I could have gone in and closed the door in his face. "I don't even know what you're talking about. Is that what MacMurray's supposed to've left with us? Money?" My right hand was so swollen and painful that I had begun to wonder if I had broken something after all. I found a pan, filled it with cold water from the tap, and dunked my hand in it. "Well, I'm sorry to disillusion you, but he didn't. Not only did he not leave any money with us, he hadn't even paid us all he owed. So go look somewhere else, okay?"

"What's wrong with your hand? It's all swollen."

"I noticed that."

"What you said, before, about finishing the job my friends started, I don't understand that. Was that you at the *ofisa?* What were you doing there?" He was standing against the door with one hand on the knob, apparently undecided whether to stay or go.

"I was trying to find out what it is MacMurray supposedly gave me that everyone wants so badly. Instead, I wound up maybe breaking my damn fool hand in an effort to save your life, God knows why, and getting jumped by a bunch of your relatives by way of thanks."

He made his decision suddenly and shut the door. "C'mon, what're you so mad at me for?" He sat at the table with the air of a man who has come home and who is prepared to be patient about a belated dinner. Slouching comfortably in his chair with his outstretched legs crossed at the ankles, one elbow on the table and his chin resting in his cupped hand, he grinned at me in sweet and perfect innocence.

"What the hell d'you think?" I gave up on the cold water, which wasn't helping much anyway, and got out the gin. "My client's been killed, my revolver confiscated by the police, my partner drugged." I found a glass and filled it with ice cubes, thought about it, and dumped it half full of straight Boodles gin. Ordinarily I don't drink it straight, but it was that kind of night. "My office, my house, and my partner's apartment have all been searched, and your sister wasn't nearly as tidy about it as you were. I've been conned, mugged, threatened, and openly shot at, all in the space of the few hours since I met you. And no, I'm not feeling real jolly about it. Did you honestly think I would?''

"But the money, you got that, don't you?" The grin was gone, replaced by a look of earnest anxiety.

"No, I do not have 'the money.' For chrissake, what money?"

"Oh." He looked at my glass. "Could I have some of that? Is it gin?"

"You've got a lot of nerve."

"I know." He smiled, relinquishing the anxiety but not the earnestness. "You said that before."

I sighed. "You must know where the glasses are. You've been in all my cupboards." I couldn't find a position that was comfortable for my bruised hand. After considerable experimentation I settled for cradling it lovingly against the opposite shoulder.

Nick got a glass and ice and poured himself a healthy slug of gin. "Let me see." He reached for my hand.

"Leave me alone, damn you." But it wasn't easy to be angry with him; he looked so contrite when I cursed him.

"Ailie, I'm sorry," he said. "Oh, jeez, I didn't, I thought she said—"

"Spit it out."

"Oh, hell, forget it."

"Fine." On second thought, resting my hand against the other shoulder wasn't too good, either. I looked at it and decided more gin was in order. My knuckles were twice their normal size and turning an ugly purplish red. And it hurt. I tried resting it over my head to reduce the throbbing, and closed my eyes, wondering why I was such a damn idiot. I knew better than to hit people in the jaw with my fist. In the movies it makes a satisfying *thwack!* and the hero prevails, but neither party is broken. In real life it doesn't make so much noise, but it's likely to break both the hand that hits and the jaw that's hit. It wasn't as if I didn't know that. I'd been here before.

Nick moved before I could stop him. He had my right forearm in a steel grip, but he wasn't looking at my hand. His strange, dark, Gypsy eyes stared straight into mine. Challenging, but with a hooded wariness. Very slowly he pulled my arm across the table till my hand was in front of him. Then, when he was sure I wasn't going to pull away, he looked down at it.

I couldn't read the expressions that crossed his face like a series of shadows. "Looks broken," he said. "What happened?"

"It was my own fault. I slugged somebody. It seemed expedient."

"Who you hit, you did that to keep her from shooting me again?"

I nodded.

"So now who's the hero?"

I pulled, and he released my hand. "There are no heroes. Only fools."

He thought about that. "What's 'expedient'?"

"Suited to the circumstances." That made him cock his head in puzzlement. I tried again. "The right thing to do."

"Oh. But to do it, you broke your hand."

"Just bruised, I think." I smiled. "Another example of how life ain't like the TV shows. If I were a P.I. on TV, hitting somebody wouldn't even skin my knuckles."

"I don't understand why you did that."

"It wasn't entirely altruistic motives. The lady had a revolver. True, she aimed it at you to start with. But by the time I hit her, she was trying to use it on me. Bruised is better than dead."

"Sonja?" He went right for the heart of the matter.

"Her I.D. says her name is Nancy Thompson."

"Sonja was trying to kill *you?*"

"That's right, sweetheart." I was beginning to feel the gin. If I had any sense, I'd stop when I begin to feel it. We've already discussed how much sense I have. I drank some more.

"But why?" His face was a comedy of confusion. I hadn't noticed before how his eyebrows slanted down away from the bridge of his nose, the way a cartoonist depicts sorrow. It added to the overall vulnerability, as if this were a man capable of shedding tears.

But he was a man. I therefore doubted he ever had shed tears. As someone wiser than I once said, the male ideal in our society has long been almost complete emotional constipation. Real men don't eat quiche. I could understand that; I didn't, either. But at least I knew how silly my macho was. "Maybe because I was trying to keep her from killing you. Maybe just because I was there. How should I know? This is all your game. I'm just an innocent bystander sucked in through misinformation. Somebody thinks I'm involved. Therefore I am involved. But I'd as soon not be."

"You really ain't got the money?"

"Alas, as I keep telling you, I don't have the money. What money?"

He ignored the question. "But Sonja said—"

"The one whose I.D. says she's Nancy Thompson?"

"Yeah, that was for the *hukkaben*. She called here, while you was gone. When it was me that answered, that surprised her. That she wasn't expecting. But what she said, she said since I answered that meant you and me really was stealing the money, you understand, and she said, she didn't want to believe that before, but—"

"This Nancy really is the same sister Sonja we met in the *ofisa* today? There aren't two women who look just alike or anything?"

He paused in his recital and gulped his gin. "Her Gypsy name is Sonja. She's my sister."

"Some family you've got."

"But if you ain't got the money, what that has to mean—"

"Nick."

He stopped.

I rubbed my eyes with my good hand. "I'm tired, and I'm getting drunk. I'm really not ready for this." I looked at him, thinking about it. "Okay. Let's start by getting one thing straight. I do not have anything of yours. If I had, I'd give it to you. I don't steal. I am, in fact, considered pathologically honest by some of my acquaintances. A disadvantage in my line of work, but I live with it. So the point is, whatever else is going on, I'm not your enemy. Hell, I don't know, I might even be your friend if you give me a chance. We have to get that settled before we go any further."

"Get what settled?" He really didn't know what I meant.

"Let's choose up sides, okay? You're on one

side. I'm not on the other. I'm either on the same side or I'm out of the game." He still didn't understand. I tried another tack. "Nick, d'you trust me?"

"'Course not." He looked at me as if I had taken leave of my senses. True, I hadn't expected an affirmative answer. I had expected a simple negative.

"Why 'of course not'? Why so adamant?"

"What's 'adamant'?"

"Never mind. Why 'of course'?"

"You're a *gadjo*."

"You can't trust anyone who isn't a Gypsy? Then who do you trust? Gypsies? Who shoot at you?"

That stopped him. After a moment he shrugged and almost smiled, pleased to've found an answer. "Me. I trust me."

"That's it?"

He nodded, still pleased. "Sure."

Suddenly I wanted to cry. I resisted the impulse, but it made my throat hurt. The poor lummox didn't have any idea there was anything wrong with that answer. "Is it like that for all Gypsies?"

He surprised me again. "'Course not!" For a long moment we stared at each other across the battered surface of my secondhand kitchen table. Then something happened in his eyes, something dark and desolate. "Gypsies," he began, and paused, and looked away from me, and tried again.

"Usually Gypsies, we trust each other. *Chachimo Romano*—the truth is said in Romany. Lying or stealing or cheating, we do that to the *gadjo,* not to each other. But to me...I am my father's son. He is not like other Gypsies." He was suddenly tired of explaining. "Would you judge the lives of all *gadje* by your own life?"

"No." I rested my aching hand against my neck. "Why do you stay with them, Nick, in spite of how they treat you? Is it just because you think Gypsies have to stick together? You feel it would be wrong to try to find another way to live?"

"I am what I am."

"You are what you choose to be. Each of us is. We have the right to choose."

"You don't choose who your parents will be. That you don't choose, your family, your language, your race."

"But you're free to choose what to do with it."

"You don't understand. It's different for the *gadje.* It ain't important to you. The tradition. The life. It ain't the same."

"Then tell me."

"I don't know how."

"Okay." I looked away, confused by the pain in his eyes. "Okay, I'm sorry." I tipped up my glass to chew on an ice cube. "So we're different. Is that it, then? You have to lie to the *gadje,* so everything you tell me is a lie?"

He looked surprised. "No, I told you the truth."

"Okay. I'll buy that. Now let me try to explain something to you." I hesitated, uncertain how to begin. "I'm not a Gypsy. I don't know anything about Gypsies. I don't really even know you. But here you are in my kitchen, and what am I going to do about that?"

"Do about it?"

"I think I like you." His glance flickered toward me and away again, as though I'd said I believed in Santa Claus. I ignored it. "I think I'd like to help you. But if I can't trust you, I can't help you. In fact, I don't even want you around."

"So I'll go." He started to rise.

Maybe I should have let him go. The thought never crossed my mind. I was in this too deep already to back out that easily now. "That isn't what I meant."

He sat back down, waiting.

"Can I trust you?"

He gave me an innocent look. I'll bet he practiced in front of mirrors. "Sure. Sure, you can trust me."

"Bull."

That startled him. "What?"

"If you don't trust me, then I can't trust you. What happens when you decide I'm working against you?"

"Then I would..."

"Yes?"

After a moment he said impatiently. "Okay, I said I'd go," and started to rise again.

"No middle ground?"

"What?"

"Sit down." He sat down. "Could we have a truce? A compact? A bargain?"

He eyed me warily. "Like what?"

"Like, if you decide I am working against you, you'll give me fair warning? You'll tell me, maybe even tell me why? Before you just go into another fit of rage and call me *gadjo* and start lying or stealing or whatever?"

He wanted to say, "Sure," just like that, lie to the *gadjo*. But he didn't. Instead, he sipped his gin, and sighed, and looked away. "I don't know."

"Nick, you're going to have to trust somebody sometime."

He shook his head stubbornly. "No."

"Just you, all alone against the world forever?"

"Always has been."

"D'you like it that way?"

Again he wanted to lie. But he didn't. "No." He looked at me then, and his eyes were terrible. "But I don't know nothing better."

"Could anything be worse?"

"No." He didn't even hesitate over that one.

"Then for chrissake, Nick, give yourself a chance. Try it. Try something new. If it can't get worse, then what've you got to lose? I'm not asking you to believe I'm perfect. I'm just asking you to give me a chance. You don't have to trust me. Just don't distrust me. There is a difference, you know.''

''I know.''

''Then do that much, and tell me when you can't anymore. That's all I'm asking.''

''Why should I?''

''Because you've got no real reason not to. And nowhere else to turn. Those are my terms. Take it or leave it.''

He grinned suddenly. ''You're one tough lady.''

''You better believe it.'' I'm a sucker for certain forms of flattery.

''Okay,'' he said. ''It's a deal.''

Maybe if I'd known then what I know now about Gypsies and how they relate to non-Gypsies, I wouldn't have believed him. But I didn't know from Gypsies. I just knew there was a desperately lonely, fiercely independent boy/man sitting at my kitchen table, and he was doing his damnedest to understand and even to accept the idea that someone might honestly befriend him for himself, and mean it. That had never happened to him before.

He had lived his whole life behind enemy lines, barricading his soul against all entry. Every time he had let his defenses down, he'd got hurt. Yet here he was, scared silly, but ready to try again. "Thank you," I said.

"All I said was I'll warn you."

"That's all I asked." I tried putting my sore hand over my head again.

"Ain't ice or something supposed to be good for bruises?"

Now I knew how he felt earlier when I was so solicitous of his injury. "Enough already. We can plan our next move in the morning. I'm too tired to think. Let's go to bed."

His eyebrows lifted. "Together?"

It wasn't what I had meant, but the idea had merit. "Sure. Why not?"

TEN

I HAD A king-sized waterbed. It was an artifact from that period in my marriage when my husband believed that if he could just find the correct material object and purchase it, all our marital problems would be solved. He also tried a color television set (when we divorced, he got that), a diamond necklace (we sold it), and a power lawn mower. I don't know what the lawn mower was supposed to do for us. The bed was obvious, and the necklace was a bribe, but a lawn mower? I liked pushing the manual mower we had before.

Anyway, you can't shore up a crumbling bridge by throwing confetti at it. The marriage still didn't work.

The bed, however, worked fine. So did Nick. I don't know what I expected, either overwhelming awkwardness or unbridled lust, I suppose. Those are the extremes one might expect with an illiterate lummox in the bedroom. Instead, he was incredibly gentle, even romantic. It had been a long time since I'd experienced that kind of lovemaking. Generally I avoided sex, both because it was becoming physically dangerous and because it always seemed to be used as a substitute for something else. Love, intimacy, friendship—whatever words were currently in vogue, the result was mutual masturbation, and I prefer doing that alone. I know just how I like it. Besides, that way I get to wake up alone in the morning. I like that, too.

When sex wasn't being used as a substitute for the things it should instead be an expression of, it was used as a simple and desperate effort to combat the natural loneliness that is the human condition. For me that just doesn't work. Sex might make me forget for a while, but so will a good book. If that's the only object, I find a book more satisfying in relation to the effort involved.

Lovemaking, however, is something different, and all too rare. Nick was a gifted practitioner. Not practiced, with that boorish, master-of-the-art attitude of men who have read all the sex manuals and tried all the positions, but attentive. We started with no assumptions and learned by paying attention.

He wasn't in a hurry. We had all the time in the world to explore each other's bodies in the warm, sweet comfort of my waterbed. He seemed to know, or quickly learn, everything that would please me. Even the hooded gaze of his dark wild eyes was a caress. They were deeper and darker than I had seen before. Eternity was just a shadow in their vast distances. They made promises, those eyes. But nothing he could not deliver.

When he smiled at me, my bones melted. There was a touch of uncertainty, a hint of awkwardness in his smile, as though he had little occasion to use it. It was as artless and as splendid as the rest of him. I felt close and comfortable with him, unselfconsciously secure, and dangerously safe in his arms.

It was still dark when I woke. At first I didn't understand what woke me. Then I heard it again: a desperate little lost-puppy sound somewhere in the darkness beside me. I remembered abruptly that I wasn't alone.

We had come untangled in our sleep. He was clear on the other side of the wide bed, curled in a protective huddle with his back to me. I flipped on the lamp and sat up. The motion rocked the waterbed, but it didn't wake him. In the nether regions of his dream the motion was somehow transformed into a threat. He reacted against it with a startled cry and lifted one arm as if to fend off a blow.

Oddly, the gesture annoyed me. This was the kind of nonsense that made up cheap melodramas, something intended to endear the tragic hero to the hearts of the audience. I hate having my heartstrings tugged, much less intentionally plucked and chorded like a musical instrument. In real life grown-ups hardly ever have nightmares, and when they do, they wake themselves, dismiss it, and go back to sleep. They don't make desperate puppy sounds and pitiful, childlike gestures of defense.

I touched his shoulder. "Nick?"

That woke him. Those fawn-soft eyes snapped open and he froze, frail and stiff as dry sticks for an instant. Then memory returned and he relaxed.

"You were dreaming."

He blinked and reached automatically for a cigarette beside the bed, didn't find one, and looked slowly around the room in dazed surprise.

"You okay now?" I asked. I couldn't maintain my irritation. This wasn't a cheap melodrama. This was Nick's life. If what he was living in was a particularly lurid soap opera, it was still real.

"Sure." His voice wasn't quite steady, but close. "Sorry, did I wake you?"

"It's okay."

He sat up. "You got any cigarettes?" He arranged his pillow against the headboard and leaned against it, eyes wide open like a child afraid of the dark and determined not to sleep.

"Sure. Here." I kept a pack in the drawer of the bedside table as an invisible defense against insomnia. I used to smoke a lot of them. They didn't cure the insomnia, but they gave me something to do while I waited for sleep to sound inviting. "They're probably stale. They've been here for a long time."

"Don't matter." He accepted the pack and a book of matches from me. Lighting one, he inhaled deeply, made a face, and glanced around for an ashtray. I handed him that, too. He put it on his lap and leaned his head against the headboard.

He obviously wasn't ready to sleep again. I arranged my pillow so I could lean against the headboard next to him and lit a cigarette for myself. They were stale.

After a while he graced me with another of his shy, lopsided smiles. "Jeez, it's quiet. You live here all by yourself?"

"I do now."

"Now?"

"Since my divorce."

He frowned. "You ain't divorced."

"Okay. I'm not divorced."

"C'mon."

"I give up. Why am I not divorced?"

"That ain't what I meant. I mean, if you say you're divorced, then okay, I believe you. It's just that, well, I guess I thought Americans didn't get married so young. You know?"

"Americans? Aren't you American?"

"No. I'm Romany."

"Oh." I hadn't realized the lines were so clearly drawn. "I was twenty-one when I married. Twenty-three when I divorced. A respectable age for each event."

"I thought you were younger than that."

"Than what? Twenty-three? I'm not. I'm considerably older. That was several years ago. Why? How old are you?" That wasn't a question I'd ordinarily have asked. I was a little surprised to hear it come out of my mouth. Age is only numbers. I thought he couldn't give me an answer that would disturb me. But he had a habit of surprising me.

"I don't know."

"How can you not know?"

"I'm maybe twenty-five, twenty-six, somewhere in there. Usually my family, they would keep track, but with me, well, what happened, I guess everybody forgot."

"Couldn't you get a copy of your birth certificate?"

He looked at me as though I had suggested a thoroughly discreditable activity. "We don't do that. Birth certificates. What we do, we just, you know, the woman takes some time off from her *boojo,* or the caravan pulls over beside the road, or whatever, and she has the baby, and they don't go to no hospitals or nothing. So there's no record. That's why nobody even knows how many Gypsies there are. We don't get all our names in some damn computer so everybody knows where we are all the time."

"And you don't celebrate birthdays?"

"Usually we do. But, I guess one time when I ran away, I was just a kid, I guess the family, they forgot. I was nine or ten or something and I had more things to worry about than when it would be my birthday. My dad, he sure didn't give a damn. Probably my mom would've kept track, only she's dead. She died while I was gone that time. That's why I went back. When I heard she was sick, you know... But I didn't get there in time. She was already dead.''

"I'm sorry."

He shrugged.

There wasn't anything more to say about that, so I got back to the point that bothered me. ''But how could a nine- or ten-year-old live, I mean, what did you do? For a living? How could you eat? Where'd you sleep?''

"Oh, wherever. It ain't no big deal. I stole food to eat, and I begged money and shined shoes and sold papers and, you know, whatever. For a while I had this neat wooden container like a shipping box or something that I lived in, but somebody stole it one day when I was out getting food.'' He said it as though it were quite an ordinary thing to live in a shipping crate, and only mildly regrettable to have one's home stolen in one's absence.

"That's appalling."

"What does that mean, appalling?"

I told him.

"What do *you* know?" He stubbed out his cigarette. "Sorry." He looked around the room, searching for something else to say. "Um, I guess you had no children? When you were married?"

"Why d'you ask?"

"I don't know."

"I have a daughter. She lives with her father."

"You didn't keep her? I mean, I would've thought…"

"What? That I would've kept her? What do *you* know?"

"I said I was sorry."

We glared at each other briefly. But there was mischief in the dark of his eyes. He'd nearly forgotten his nightmare, and he knew full well I wasn't really angry. I gave up and grinned at him. "So you did. Okay. I didn't keep her because I knew I wasn't going to remarry and settle down and make a comfy little home for a kid. I'm not the mothering type. I should've figured that out before I produced a child, but I didn't, and better late than never, I figure. My husband married a woman who is precisely the mothering type, and my daughter is very happy with them. I see her sometimes in the summer. She thinks I'm a maiden aunt. Do I shock you?"

"Did you want to?"

"For an illiterate Gypsy lummox, you're pretty damn perceptive."

"Told you, I ain't clumsy, so I ain't no lummox. What's 'perceptive'?"

"Never mind. I'm not a damn dictionary, for chrissake. Besides, you're too sexy to argue with." I leaned over to nibble his earlobe, and when he least expected it, I tickled him.

He caught me, pinned me down, and tickled me relentlessly. I couldn't squirm away. Perhaps my heart wasn't in the effort. I hadn't heard him laugh before. It was a pure, clean sound of delight.

We both sobered at the same instant. For a long moment he stared into my eyes, a curious look of wonder and maybe something like love. Abruptly he kissed me, with such fierce passion, such awful need, that I forgot everything but the hard, hungry pressure of his body against mine.

We made love again, more sweet and sure than the first time, as if our bodies had already learned to fill the curves and hollows of each other's need. I fell asleep afterward exhausted but content, and wondered only briefly whether I would manage to wake up as early in the morning as I intended. I wanted to get to the office before the building opened so I could jimmy the lock on the office door. That way when I reported the theft of the MacMurray file to the police I wouldn't have to admit I knew about it when it happened but didn't bother to report it till morning.

ELEVEN

I DID WAKE early, and I tried to slip out of bed without disturbing Nick. Although he didn't say anything, I saw the glitter of his open eyes in the half-dark of the bedroom as I closed the door on my way to the bathroom, and I think I really expected to find him gone when I came out of the shower. Instead, I found him in the kitchen. He had got out my old aluminum griddle and raided my refrigerator, and there was bacon, crisp and aromatic, already waiting beside the sizzling skillet. An egg in his hand, he glanced at me as I appeared in the kitchen doorway.

"How many eggs?" he asked. Outside, the eastern sky was white with the rising dawn, and the dark hills were like thunderclouds still gemmed with strings of streetlights, orange above Berkeley and palest green everywhere else. Soon early morning commuters would break the silence with the sound of their starting cars, but now the street belonged to the last swift shadows of the night.

"Two, please." I was surprised to see Nick so competent in the kitchen, but I wasn't going to question it. I was too hungry to take the chance.

The coffee was ready, so I poured two cups and took them to the table. I had towel-dried my hair and applied some hasty makeup. A dab of lipstick, some eyeliner, and mascara. The basic necessities. I do it more for my sake than for anyone else's. I look acceptable without. I feel attractive with. That's the deciding factor. How you feel you look is at least as important as how you really do look. Maybe more important.

While he fried our eggs, I gulped some coffee and went back to the bedroom to find a clean dress. It was going to be hot again today. When the sun is still climbing the eastern hills and already there's no fog to shelter the Bay Area cities from the summer sky, it's going to be hot. But I had to deal with the police today, so I wanted to look demure. I chose a light cotton print sundress with white eyelet ruffles and a modest neckline. It required underwear, but I could tolerate that. I found a pair of sturdy sandals that could take a lot of walking, just in case. It was becoming clear that Nick's Gypsies were involved in my life whether I liked it or not. I wanted to be ready for just about anything.

After a moment's hesitation I went to the bedroom and got out Sharon's birthday present, removed the neat giftwrap the store had obligingly encased it in, and strapped it on. It was a holster for her .22 that would conceal it against the right thigh just above the knee. My skirt ended just be-

low the knee, so with some minimal caution of
movement I could keep the holster hidden. The .22
was easier to reach and less easy to get parted from
there than it would be in my purse.

Nick was buttering toast for me when I returned
to the kitchen. The eggs shared a plate with bacon
and one already buttered slice of toast. His eggs
were on the stove. "You're quite a handy housewife." I let up the shades so we could watch the
changing light in the sky.

"I forgot to ask you how you wanted your eggs.
They're over easy, is that okay?"

"Super. D'you do this often, or is it an act of
atonement for something?"

He turned away to tend his eggs. "What's
'atonement'?"

I kept forgetting. "Never mind. That was just an
extraordinarily stupid way of saying thanks."

"You're welcome." About to serve his eggs, he
paused to appraise my appearance. "You going
somewhere?"

"I have an office to tend."

"Oh." He returned the skillet to the stove.

"Is something wrong?"

His toast popped up and he lifted it from the
toaster, sucked in his breath as it singed his fingers,
and passed it from hand to hand on the way to the
table. "No. Yes. I don't know."

"I'm not walking out on you, Nick."

"I don't need nobody's help."

"I know that. But like it or not, I am involved in this mess. Certain relatives of yours believe I am possessed of money that belongs to them. Something about a *hukkaben* I think you said. Whatever that is."

"You'd call it a hustle, I think." He sat down and picked up his fork. "It's no big deal. Sonja found this guy MacMurray that had a lot of money and he liked her, so she got all that I.D. as Nancy Thompson so he'd think she was a rich *gadjo*, and she promised to marry him. They opened a joint checking account to pay for the wedding and the honeymoon and everything. He thought they were both putting in a lot of money, you understand. All she did is, she took out his money and she came to California."

"So where do I fit in? Why do they think I have the money? She stole it from MacMurray and then he's supposed to have given it to me? That doesn't make sense." The eastern sky was brightening, its lucent blue deepening, and the hills had transformed themselves from flat, gemmed black to molded velvet, encrusted from base to crest with close-packed white boxes that the rising sun, when it reached its long fingers over the hills, would wash in palest gold and oblique shadows.

Nick shook his head. "Before, Sonja told my little sister Lela that I had the money. She said she gave it to me while we was all in Chicago, right after the *hukkaben* you understand, and she said I was supposed to bring it out here but I didn't. That's what she told Lela, so Lela, she wanted me to send enough money to buy herself out of this marriage.''

''And did Sonja give you the money in Chicago?''

'''Course not. Only thing I had to do with the family in Chicago was I went to visit, because I wanted to see my sister Lela, and my father, he found me there and he got me cornered and he beat the shit out of me, him and some of his buddies that probably believed whatever lies he told them about me because he is my father. I never even saw Lela, or Sonja either, so when would she give me this money? When I woke up, they was all gone.''

''Coming here? From Chicago? And you followed them? Why?''

''I didn't follow them right away. But then it was like I told you. Lela wanted the money, the brideprice you understand, and I didn't have the *hukkaben* money, but if she thought I did, that meant either my father had already spent it or else Sonja's hiding it somewhere. I came to see if I could get enough of it from them to pay back Lela's brideprice for her.'' He seemed to see nothing out of the ordinary about discussing stolen money and purchased people over the breakfast table.

"And you tried to steal my car so you could find out where I lived and search my house for the money." I looked at him. "But what in the world made you think I'd have it? How could I have got it?"

"From MacMurray. Sonja told me you had it. When I phoned the *ofisa* that morning, she told me. And that night, while you were gone, she called here, to see if you were gone so she could search your place. So then she told me how MacMurray got the money from her to leave it with you. He killed Auntie Tia and threatened to kill Sonja if she didn't give it to him. So she gave it to him. And she said he left it with you. For safekeeping." His long fingers wrapped themselves too tightly around his coffee cup. I couldn't read his eyes; his hair hid them from me like a veil.

"Nick, that's ridiculous. He wouldn't give it to me for safekeeping, he'd give it to a bank. And even if he would...if that's when he got the money, when did he give it to me? You were with me all the time from when we found the body—I assume that was Auntie Tia?—till you searched my house."

He studied the remains of his breakfast. "I thought maybe..." He shrugged. "I don't know what I thought. Sonja said she started the *hukkaben* all over again when she gave him the money. She was going to meet him at the El Cerrito BART station to run away with him. He could have left the money here while you were gone.'' He lifted his gaze to me hopefully, as though he thought it possible I might yet reach into some unsuspected pocket about my person and pull out his family's money with a flourish and a smile.

"But he wouldn't have. He didn't. Nick, I've never seen this money. And if MacMurray had it when he died, somebody else has it now. The cops would've mentioned if they'd found it with him.''

He studied the remains of his breakfast. "Sonja sent my father after MacMurray, and another man who is my father's friend. But they didn't find the money.''

"They killed him?''

He shrugged, his eyes shadowed, his mouth a grim and bitter line. The morning light cast his face in stone, pale and still and beautiful. "Of course. My father, he acts like a *gadjo* sometimes.''

I let that pass. "This doesn't make sense, Nick. What makes you think Sonja doesn't still have the money, herself? Isn't that what you were looking for at the *ofisa?*''

"No, I was looking for Lela's bride-price that her husband paid to my father. If he hadn't spent it, I could have given it back to the husband's family. That would be more than fair. He beats her, you understand, so it would be right to pay back only half. But the bride-price wasn't in the chair where my sister Sonja told me my father kept it. Probably, what my father did, he has already spent it, or he might have lost it at the races.''

"So now you're back to looking for the *hukkaben* money. I don't have it, Nick. MacMurray didn't leave it with me.''

He pushed at his breakfast plate, then picked it up and rose to carry it to the sink. "You have a partner,'' he said when his back was to me. Nor did he turn to face me again until I had responded.

"He didn't leave it with Sharon, either.'' Conscious of his listening stillness, I said impatiently, "She'd have told me.'' He turned then, to study me with those serious dark eyes. I said, "I think Sonja must still have the money. But, Nick, even if we find it, it belongs to MacMurray's heirs. You can't use it to buy your little sister.''

He took my plate and put it with his in the sink. "The money don't belong to MacMurray's what-you-saids. MacMurray, he stole it, you understand. From his place of work. Do you want more coffee?''

"Then it belongs to his place of work. Yes, please.''

He poured for both of us, shaking his head stubbornly as he did it. "I need that money to pay Lela's husband's family.'' He returned the pot to the fire and sat down. "But what I don't understand, if Sonja, she has the money, if she never gave it to nobody, then when she tore up your office and your friend's apartment like you said, what was she looking for there?'' His voice was subdued, but there was challenge in his tone.

"I don't know." I gestured helplessly. "That's not the only unanswered question. This whole thing's crazy." I stared out the window at the brightening hills. "I don't believe MacMurray killed that woman we found at the *ofisa*. He wasn't the killing kind. At least, not that way. Not just as a random show of force.''

He shifted uncomfortably and lifted his coffee, then put it down without drinking. "But if Auntie Tia saw Sonja get the money from hiding, which she had claimed all along she didn't have, and if she saw her give it to MacMurray…" He hesitated.

"Then she could tell the whole family Sonja had it all along," I said. "Sonja wouldn't like that. And my guess is, she is the killing kind." I sipped my coffee. "But that would mean she did give it to MacMurray. I don't understand why she would. There's more going on here. What about those guys that jumped me last night outside the *ofisa?* Where do they fit in? And how did I manage to fend off all three? The more I think about it, the more I think I'm not exactly that good. Oh, I don't mean I didn't hurt them, because I did, but maybe they were pulling their punches. Seemed to me even at the time they were a little slow.''

Unexpectedly, Nick grinned. "Probably they were surprised you could fight, is all. Usually Gypsy women, they don't fight like that."

"Like what? You mean you saw it?"

"Sure."

"And you didn't help me?"

"I didn't know it was you. Besides, you didn't seem to need no help."

"Oh." I wasn't sure whether that was flattering or not. "That means you saw them. Who were they? Did you recognize them? Do you have any idea why they would have jumped me like that?"

"Those, they were friends of Sonja's. A cousin, an uncle, another I didn't know. Probably what it was, they were waiting for me. Maybe Sonja, she told them I might be there. Then maybe when they saw you come out of the *ofisa*, or maybe they knew who you are, you know—Sonja, she could've told them you got the money. I don't know. I didn't wait to ask no questions."

"No, neither did I." I sighed. "What we're left with is, your relatives still think I have the money—how much is it, anyway?"

"A hundred thousand."

"That was going to be some wedding!"

"And the honeymoon, you understand. Sonja, she can act like a rich *gadjo* real good."

"I guess. A hundred thousand dollars. They'll be

after me, all right. I'd be after me, too, in their place."

"What I could do, I could tell them you ain't got the money, that you never got it from Mac-Murray."

"You think they'd believe you?"

"Maybe."

He meant it. Maybe they were as unpredictable to him as they were to me. Maybe when you're dealing with unpredictable people you have all the more options. Like telling them the truth when they've no reason to believe it is the truth. "Then that might be a place to start."

"Sure."

"Meanwhile, I've got curious. I wonder where the money really is?"

There was a silence while he thought about it. The morning sun burst finally up over the distant hills and cast a sudden shaft of copper-gold through my kitchen window that spun a brilliant nimbus over the storm-black of Nick's tousled hair and gilded one side of his face till he lifted one hand to shade his eyes. "MacMurray was a *gadjo*," he said, in a tone that hinted worlds of mystery. "Who can say?" He glanced at me, remembering, perhaps, that I was *gadjo* too. "Where would a *gadjo* put his money, in a hurry, if he wanted to keep it from someone such as my family?"

"In a bank, I should think."

He shook his head. His hair sparked black fire in the light. "Not a bank."

"Why not a bank? It makes more sense than giving it to me. He didn't know me well enough to trust me with one hundred thousand dollars."

"This *gadjo*, he wanted to be able to get to the money fast, any time of day. Probably he believed Sonja, you know, because he did want to marry her, so he would want to believe her, too. But he was not a stupid man. He had trusted her once. He would have hesitated a second time. So what he wanted, he wanted the money out of his hands in case she sent somebody besides herself to meet him, but he wanted it where he could get it if she did come. If he gave it to you, what he might have done, he might have packaged it in some way, and he might not have told you what was inside the package." His voice was half hopeful, half resigned.

"He didn't give me a package, Nick. I'm sorry. And I'd know if he'd given one to Sharon."

"He would not use a bank. Then he could not get to it readily enough, you understand."

I thought about that. "Then could it have been in his car? Did anybody search the car?"

He lifted his head, blinking against the light, to determine which windowshade would shield him, then rose to pull it down, casting a cool oblong of shadow across the table. "My father," he said, "he is an evil man, but he is not a fool. And he is a thief. Even if Sonja didn't tell him MacMurray had the money—which how could she, if she would have the family believe I have it—my father, he would search the car.''

''Thoroughly?'' I asked. He nodded. ''Then I can't imagine. Everybody's been double-crossing everyone else in this whole business. Maybe if Sonja did give MacMurray the money, your father found it and kept it for himself.''

Nick stared at me, scandalized. ''My father, he would not steal from the Gypsies.''

''That's what you would've said about your sister Sonja a few days ago.''

TWELVE

I GAVE NICK a ride to Berkeley, and didn't ask where he was going from there, or whether he would be back. There was a precarious tension between us, born of last night's intimacy and this morning's conversation. I don't have any idea what he was thinking. What I was thinking was confused to the point of idiocy. I was fonder of him than I wanted to admit; I didn't trust him any farther than I could see him; I wanted to go back to bed with him at once, no waiting; and I more than half wished I had called the cops when I first saw him trying to steal my car. As a rule, I am a practical and prosaic sort of person, not given to romantic flights of fancy or prey to girlish infatuations. Finding myself suddenly subject to both, I didn't know how to react or what to do about it. I took the easy course. I did nothing about it.

The sun was climbing the sky above the hills, a brilliant circle burned in the luminous blue, and the city was coming awake by the time we reached Berkeley. I let Nick off at the corner of Shattuck and University and went on around the block to park in the alley behind the office building. There was a plump, dark-haired bag lady digging ambitiously in the Dumpster at the base of the rubbish chute who glanced up and went on talking to herself as I got out of the car. No one else saw me go in.

It didn't take long to jimmy the lock on our office door. The wood was crumbling with age and dry rot. I left by the back stairs again to avoid any ambitious secretaries who might show up early, returned to my Capri, and had to identify a curious sense of relief at finding it where I'd left it.

I hadn't taken out the rotor arm. It occurred to me, as I pulled out of the alley, that had been a deliberate, cheap, and meaningless test of Nick's attitude toward me. Would he steal from me? Was he being honest with me? Did he, I could hear the girlish question in my mind, *care* for me? For chrissake, you'd think I was a teenager in search of a husband. I'd had my fun with Nick last night. If that was all there was, it was still more than I'd been looking for. I wouldn't turn down a longer relationship with him, but I wasn't in the market for a permanent relationship with anyone. I couldn't handle permanent relationships. I knew; I'd tried.

It was still early when I got to Sharon's apartment, but she was up and functioning and a good deal more rational today. I stood at her kitchen window with morning sun hot on my back and filled her in on all the events she'd missed, leaving out only those details I considered too personal to report. She guessed that part with no trouble at all.

"You're in love with him." Like Nick, she struck right to the heart of a matter.

"I wouldn't say that."

She studied me a moment, then shrugged. "You're trying not to be in love with him." She was dressed already, in a green halter top and matching pants, and had rearranged her apartment to a state of tidiness probably in excess of that which Sonja had destroyed. Now she was standing barefoot on the cracked linoleum floor of her shiny-clean kitchen, offering me coffee and pouring some for herself as well. The "compleat detective." Unfazed by yesterday's adventures, unrattled by chaos, she'd obviously been up for several hours and spent the time methodically righting the wrongs of yesterday that she could reach—which meant, cleaning her apartment.

"Get serious," I said. "He'd turn any heterosexual woman's knees weak just to look at him, but sex isn't everything."

"Maybe not, but it's everything else." She wiped an invisible spot from the counter top.

"That quote is supposed to be about money."

"That, too. Sit down, why don't you? The cleanliness of my apartment may be unfamiliar, but it won't attack. What are you going to do about it?"

I sat, and wrapped my hands around my coffee cup in unconscious imitation of Nick. When I realized what I was doing, I let go of it abruptly, wiped my hands hard on the sides of my skirt, and looked innocently at Sharon. "About what? The cleanliness? The money? Nick?"

"Any of the above." She was taking the coffeepot apart and washing the grounds down the sink.

"I don't know yet." I picked up my coffee, looked at it, and put it down again; I'd had enough coffee already this morning.

"I don't know either, but we have to do something." She dried her hands on a paper towel and put it in the wastebasket under the sink. Even the wastebasket looked freshly scrubbed. "I have a score to settle with this Sonja person." She closed the cupboard doors and surveyed the sparkling kitchen with satisfaction. "That may be my only vested interest, but it is vested."

"What's 'vested'?" I said it without thinking, and regretted it at once.

"What?"

"Never mind. Maybe you're right."

"About what?"

About sex, I thought. "About your vested interest," I said. "First I'm going to call the cops. I have to tell the Berkeley cops the office was rifled, so they'll verify to the El Cerrito cops that the file could have been stolen. Otherwise they're going to think I'm playing games.''

"And you're not?" She sat at the table opposite me, watching me much too alertly. The green of her costume matched the green of her eyes.

"Not the games they might think."

She thought about that. "Listen, who does this money belong to? I mean, if anyone finds it?" Her tone was elaborately casual.

"I don't know. Nick says MacMurray stole it from his 'place of work.'''

"Where's that?"

"He didn't say. But wherever it is, I suppose the money belongs to them. If anyone finds it."

"I'll check that out." She was always quicker than I to see where the potential profit was. "And I'll check out the banks. To see if I can find out whether he did open an account with it. That is the sensible place to stash money, after all."

"It's worth checking, anyway."

"Of course it is. Eliminate the obvious, first. Then, let's see, we ought to find out who killed that woman in Oakland, Nick's aunt or whoever she was. We want to find the money, I want to settle with Sonja, and you want to work something out with Nick." She ticked each item off on elegant fingers, then looked at me. "Am I leaving anything out?"

I decided it wasn't worthwhile to argue the part about Nick. "Just one small item."

"What?"

"I'd like to know who killed our client. And I think it would be a good idea if the police knew, too. Otherwise, they may continue to harbor suspicions about me. Or us."

"You're convinced Sonja did it?" She examined her fingernails, presumably checking for chipped enamel. They were painted opaque lavender, and the one on her left ring finger sported three tiny rhinestones in a decorative line near the tip.

"Either Sonja or her father. I explained all that."

"It was a logical progression of thought."

I knew that tone. "But?"

"But it's all circumstantial." She abandoned her nails and peered into her coffee with the intensity of one in search of enlightenment, or insects.

"Well, fine. We're not a court of law. Anyway, we can work on getting hard evidence."

"That wasn't what I meant." Apparently finding nothing untoward in her coffee, she drained it and put the cup down. "I don't care whether it'll hold up in court."

"What, then?"

"Aren't you going to drink your coffee?"

"No. I had some before I left home. You want it?"

"Yes." She pushed her own cup aside and

pulled mine across the table to study its contents. "I just wonder if you've, um, considered all the angles? Isn't it possible you might have, well, overlooked some possibilities?"

I saw what she was getting at, and I didn't like it. I had a neat little theory, and I didn't want to see the holes in it, mostly because I didn't like what I might see through those holes. Maybe sex wasn't everything, but I *liked* Nick. I looked at her, trying to keep my expression blank. Just because I understood her perfectly didn't mean I had to admit I did. "Meaning?"

"You got all your information from Nick."

There it was, right out loud in front of God and everybody. I got all my information from Nick. Nick the car thief, the con artist, the Gypsy who had told me in plain English that Gypsies routinely lie to *gadje*. "That reminds me," I said cravenly. "I'd also like to help rescue his little sister from this 'husband' who beats her. I don't like people who beat up little girls."

She accepted the change of subject. "I don't like people who beat up anybody, but you can't go around rescuing everybody who needs it."

"We can always try, just when it's convenient."

"Rescuing people is never convenient. Is your Gypsy going to pay for our services?"

"He's not my Gypsy."

"In other words, he's not going to pay for our services."

"He doesn't have any money."

"So he says. Hell, you don't even know if he really has a little sister named Lela whose husband beats her." She waved a negligent hand impatiently at my expression. "I'm serious, Ailie. Even if she does exist, you can't go around trying to rescue everybody that somebody says needs to be rescued."

She was right. "Why not?"

"Because there's too damn many people in need of rescue, that's why. Christ, Ailie, you're such a sucker. We have to make a living, and you don't do that by spending half your time saving the universe."

"I'm not asking for the universe here. Just one little girl."

"Who may or may not exist." She made an expansive gesture. The rhinestones threw a shower of miniature rainbows across the table. "Okay, okay," she said. "If it's convenient, we'll rescue the kid. If she exists, and if she wants to be rescued. Okay?"

"Thanks, Sharon."

"Go call the cops." She tried to sound irritated, but it didn't quite come off. Secretly she wanted to save the universe, too. "Meantime I'll check up on Nick's story, and see if I can find out where that hundred thousand dollars came from, where it belongs, and where it is now. If it exists.'' She grinned at my reaction to that. ''Get out of here.''

I went.

THIRTEEN

I USED THE front door into the office building this time. And just to be on the safe side, I took the antiquated elevator up to our floor, so the antiquated operator could verify my arrival time. I was being paranoid, but when you're dealing with cops it's best to cover all the angles, however unlikely. The operator, vexed at being made to work, did not rise to my conversational gambits. He had a little closet on the ground floor where he kept a television for entertainment during the slow hours, which he clearly hoped would be perpetual, and I must have torn him away from a really compelling program. He took a long time answering my ring, scowled at me when he got there, and grunted savagely in response to my greeting.

At my floor he dragged the doors open with an elaborate show of difficulty and ushered me off. I thanked him for the ride, but he didn't respond. Perhaps he didn't hear me. Or perhaps he was too intent on getting back to his television to notice what he heard. I left him and went down the corridor to the office.

When I had jimmied the door earlier, I hadn't

even looked inside. I thought I was accustomed to the idea that our office had been assaulted. I was wrong. The first thing I saw when I stepped inside were the two dirty coffee cups, side by side on the little table in front of the couch, and I wasn't prepared.

They were just ordinary ceramic coffee cups. Sharon's was the same chipped blue mug she once threw in the face of a would-be assassin to save my life. It still bore the splotchy remnants of the fingernail-polish initial she put on it years ago, to remind me to wash my own cup and use it instead of hers. It was a familiar, prosaic, innocuous piece of office background, symbolic of the commonplace of daily routine. At the sight of it, I realized all over again how damn close Sonja had been, how easily she could have dispatched Sharon with the same brutal, indifferent efficiency she or her father had used on our client. I shuddered, remembering Nick's insistence that Gypsies didn't commit murder. The thought should have been a warning; apparently, some Gypsies did.

But I wasn't concentrating on Nick's possible honesty then. I was too busy fighting down a weak, sick horror at what could have happened to Sharon yesterday. Death was always just two steps away in our business, but that was only one step nearer than it was in anybody's line of work. Accountants died in auto accidents every day. Waitresses fell down stairs. Filing clerks had heart attacks. Nobody lives forever. The ultimate culmination of life is death.

It was only after the fact that one thought about it: after a narrow squeak, a close call, a near thing. Then it didn't matter how common it was, or how impersonal. And in this case it didn't matter that Sharon had helped Sonja along by committing one of the ten deadly errors—she had relaxed too soon in the presence of a stranger who could be, and was, an adversary. That was irrelevant. What mattered was that one of us had cheated death one more time.

I believe one only gets so many chances. Death will be cheated only so many times. I'm not a fatalist in the sense that I think our lives are ruled by statistics and it will one day be "my turn," but I do believe there's a limit to the number of lucky breaks anybody's going to get. The next one could be the last.

The last one could be the last. Nancy Thompson or Sonja Gypsy or whatever the hell her name was chose not to kill my partner last night, but she came too damn close for comfort. Now she had a debt to pay. The gratification I received from last night's punch in the jaw was just a down payment. But that was a personal matter. I took the cups down to the ladies' room to wash them while I waited for the cops to respond to my call.

Sharon and I hadn't discussed how we were going to handle the matter of Sonja; we didn't have to. One of the things that made our partnership work was that we thought so much alike. Right now neither of us knew, beyond a vague but directional fury, what we wanted to do about Sonja. But something would present itself, and when it did, we would recognize it. Meanwhile, it had nothing to do with the police. That was why I was going out of my way to convince them I didn't know who had ransacked the office.

I had just put the cups away and was standing in the middle of the room, thinking with despair of the cleanup job ahead of me, when two of Berkeley's finest showed up to investigate my report. "Berkeley Brownshirts," the underground called them, because their uniforms were brown then; but it was an unwarranted insult. It is a hazardous and too damn unrewarding job cops do, and it carries with it certain pitfalls and prejudices no police force can fully avoid. But Berkeley did better than most.

The two who came to the office that morning were young and friendly and helpful. The woman tended toward a certain bossy superiority over both me and her partner, but it's a harder job for a woman, and the balance between authority and approachability can be difficult to find. The interview didn't take long. It was a case with obviously no leads. They promised to send along someone to lift whatever fingerprints could be found, but it was a pacifying gesture.

"Don't bother," I said. "I more than likely ruined any available fingerprints when I checked to see what, if anything, was missing."

"You shouldn't have touched anything," said the woman.

"I know as well as you do that since I can't give you any leads and since nothing of any value was taken, by tomorrow morning this case will be filed in somebody's inactive drawer."

"But the fingerprints—"

"When was the last time anybody used fingerprints to trace a suspect? They're good for identifying a suspect you've already caught, but who's gonna make a wild run through the files to match up fingerprints on a B and E where the only thing missing is a file of dubious value to anybody including me?"

Both admitted I had a point, but were reluctant to go so far as to say I was right. Instead, the man said kindly, "You understand we'll give your case the same priority we'd give any other case."

The woman sabotaged his efforts by adding rather pointedly, "What happens after we turn it over to Burglary is out of our hands."

"I know it is," I said. "Don't worry about it. If I turn up any leads, I'll turn them over to the department. Then if nothing happens, maybe I'll complain." I wouldn't, of course; there was still nothing missing, so this crime would never be high on anybody's list of priorities except mine. And I didn't need the cops' help to deal with it. They would not have approved of my methods.

When they were gone I called my friend in Burglary and asked him to convey the news of my B and E, when it came in, to the proper authorities in El Cerrito.

"Breaking and entering?" he repeated. "What's going on, Ailie? You got a rogue client?" His grin was audible.

"I don't have a client. Somebody turned his lights out. The same somebody, I think, who stole his file from my office. But don't ask me who, 'cause I don't know. Yet."

"You'll let me know when you have the case solved?"

He was a friend, but we got along better if we didn't talk business. "I'll let you know. Give ECPD a call for me, okay? That's all I ask."

"As soon as the report comes in," he promised.

"Thanks." We chatted briefly about the weather. That's usually a safe topic, and actually a valid one in the Bay Area, where if two people are far enough apart to telephone instead of shouting, they are probably experiencing different weather conditions. The heat wave eliminated some of that variability, but it provided conversation in itself. After agreeing, with suitable exclamations of surprise and disapproval, that the temperature was and had been altogether higher than could be borne by civilized beings, we ended our conversation with expressions of mutual esteem. Then I began cleaning the office.

I'd barely got the job started when Nick walked in. He startled me, since I wasn't expecting anyone. He paused in the doorway to survey the mess, then glanced nervously at me. His face was a gaunt region of shadows, wholly unreadable. "My sister Sonja, she did this?" he asked.

"She sure as hell did." Cleanup has never been one of my favorite activities. I get surly when faced with a lot of it.

"Can I help you?" He was standing still, with his hands in his pockets, and looked as though any sudden movement would make him explode. There was always an aura of tension about him, and nervousness intensified it.

"What're you so uptight about?"

"Nothing." He looked at the floor. "So you gonna let me help or what?" He bent over to pick up a file folder.

I glared at him. "You certainly can't sort files. How the hell can you survive without being able to read?"

He didn't answer me. He was looking past me at the doorway, his face impassive, his posture coiled-spring ready, his eyes dark with hooded wariness. I glanced over my shoulder in sudden alarm, ready for anything.

Sharon closed the door behind her as silently as she had opened it. I don't know how she did that. She could even open my rusted old back gate at home without a sound. It amused her to do it, because she knew I couldn't. She grinned at us cheerily. "Hi."

"Hi yourself." I handed her the stack of files I'd been collecting. "Here, sort these or something. I hate cleaning."

"I know you do. This must be Nick. Hi. I'm Sharon."

"Ailie's partner," he said. "I know." It had not escaped him that Sharon was beautiful. "I'm sorry my sister Sonja did this thing to you." His nervousness was undiminished, but now it was complicated by awe and an unexpected tendency toward subservience.

"I heard she did worse to you."

He shrugged. Getting shot was a minor inconvenience, a mere misunderstanding between friends. "She is my sister."

Sharon nodded soberly. "That explains it."

"Sharon is going to help us rescue Lela," I said brightly.

Sharon gave me the look that remark deserved; she had not said she would help. Nick didn't notice.

Mention of Lela had, by a miracle, dragged his attention from her. "For that," he said, "we got to find the money. We got to pay back half her bride-price."

"Oh, nonsense," said Sharon. "You said the husband is beating her. Nobody has to put up with that. She should leave him." She put the files I had given her on the desk. "I would be glad to help her, if she needs help. But there is the little matter of the rent."

"When we find the money, that'll pay your rent," said Nick. "I would give it to you, you understand." That was news to me. "All I need is enough to buy Lela back. I don't care about the rest."

"That money must belong to someone," I said.

They both ignored me. "Just how much does your little sister cost?" asked Sharon.

"One thousand dollars," he said proudly.

"Costly little treasure, isn't she?" said Sharon.

Nick was not good at recognizing sarcasm. "She is a good pickpocket, you understand. And she is learning the *hukkaben*. She will make a good living for a husband." His face darkened. "But not for the bastard my father sold her to."

"If he abuses her, why doesn't she just leave?"

"It would not be right. The family must have half the bride-price paid back. Besides, they will not let her leave. It is not only the boy who beats her. The family is not a good family.''

"Then why pay for her?" I asked. "Why not just take her back?"

"Because you don't know where she is, do you, Nick?" said Sharon.

"I think my sister Sonja, she knows.'' He blinked. "But I'm not sure where she is, either."

"She's not at the *ofisa?*" I asked.

"She wasn't, when I went there this morning to find her."

"It's still worth a try," said Sharon. "We'll go there first."

I looked at her. "We? So you are going to help?"

She grinned. "Maybe we'll find the money."

"It must belong to somebody," I said again.

She shook her head. "I checked. MacMurray has no surviving relatives, and the 'place of work' from which he stole it is not the kind of place that's going to be asking a lot of questions."

"What kind of place is that?"

"A house of prostitution."

"He was a *pimp?*"

"He was a bookkeeper. For a house of prostitution."

"I hate getting on the wrong side of the mob."

"It's an independent organization, with no influence at all outside Chicago. Let's go."

"You don't know we'll find the money."

"You don't know we won't."

"Admit it. You want to save the universe."

"A little good karma never hurt anybody." She led the way through the door Nick was holding open for us, turned to lock it behind us, and paused with her key in the lock when she saw the damage I had done to the door frame. The lock would be useless until that was repaired. She glanced at me but didn't say anything; instead, she scowled at Nick and said sharply, "I didn't say you could come along."

"I'm coming," he said.

She studied his face, gave an almost imperceptible shrug, and said, "Right. Come along." She was good at making the inevitable sound like it was her idea in the first place.

We did not take the elevator, for which I was grateful. I could not have faced that ancient attendant twice in one morning. We clattered down the wide stairs side by side, with Nick in the middle and leaning, in my opinion, toward Sharon's side. It was inevitable. She was shockingly beautiful, and he was a healthy male. I decided that since I had a partner like her, it was a very good thing I preferred living alone. Then I laughed at myself and returned to reality. Nick wasn't really showing a particular preference for Sharon, and I had no claim on him in any case. I was just in a foul mood, eager to find a grievance with someone. Better I should save my energy for Sonja; she was more deserving than either of these two, both of whom I liked very much.

The sun beat down steadily on the sidewalk outside, fulfilling its morning promise of another heatwave day. There had been no question, really; the end of the heat wave, when it finally came, would be heralded by foghorns one evening as chill air drifted back in from the ocean, cooled the hot air over the land, and translated its muggy humidity into fog. There had been no foghorns last night.

We took both cars, Nick in mine and Sharon following in hers. I still liked the scent of his aftershave. We drove through the still of the morning in companionable silence all the way to Oakland, where the unremitting sun seemed even hotter, trapped as the heat was between more and bigger buildings with even fewer patches of baked grass, straggling trees, or wilted bushes to give an impression of some connection with the cool, dark places of the earth.

There were two empty parking places on San Pablo right across the street from the *ofisa*. That should have been a clue; good luck always arrives in small doses. The *ofisa* itself was closed, dark, and deserted. After pounding on the door for a while and discussing and discarding the possibility of breaking in, the three of us trooped back across the street to the cars to consider our next move.

The only clue we had to Sonja's whereabouts was the hotel name and room number I had found in her purse the night before.

"Good," said Sharon. "We'll go there."

"What if she comes back here while we're gone?"

"What I could do," said Nick, "I could stay here to watch for her."

"Right," said Sharon. "You'd be real inconspicuous, leaning against the doorjamb."

"She wouldn't see me if I didn't want her to."

"You'd want her to, though, wouldn't you?" I said. "You'd confront her without us, and what the hell good would that do you?"

He looked at me, looked across the street at the *ofisa* doorway, looked at his feet. "Maybe she'd tell me where Lela is." He said it without much conviction.

"Maybe she'd kill you," I said.

"Maybe she'd try," he said.

"Maybe you should stay here with him, Ailie," said Sharon. She wasn't quite impatient with us yet, but she was getting there.

"Oh, no. I'm the one who found the hotel key."

"You're also the one who got us into this." She waved away my response to that. "Okay, okay. I'll stay here, you go check the hotel. Just find out whether she's still got a room there. If she has, that's probably a better place to wait for her than this is, so come back and let me know, either way. Meantime I'll just keep an eye on the *ofisa*.''

"What if she comes back here? And then leaves again?''

"Then I'll follow her.''

"And do what?'' Nick sounded belligerent.

"I don't know yet. Go on, get out of here. Let's not play 'what if' all day.''

We went. Sonja's hotel was a dismal old building just off San Pablo, not far from the *ofisa*, that advertised room rates by the hour, by the day, and by the week. The prices were within reason for winos. The desk clerk was asleep, or dead. The corridors were infested with self-confident cockroaches and whole armies of ants. The carpet smelled of stale urine with overtones of vomit. If Sonja had a hundred thousand dollars to play with, and stayed here anyway, there was something wrong with her mind.

Nick betrayed his nervousness only by asking me her room number three times on the way up the dark, uncarpeted stairs. When we reached the right floor he forgot I was there. Illiterate or not, he could read room numbers. He led me straight to her door and began to bang on it before I could stop him. "Sonja? You in there? Open up! Sonja!'' His shouts must've awakened drowsy winos all down the corridor.

I shoved him forcibly aside. "Nick, cool it. We

don't even know she's still renting this room." I pressed my ear, reluctantly, against the grimy surface of the door in time to hear a window inside being thrust open and the rattling sounds of hard-soled shoes climbing out onto the fire escape. "It's Sonja," I said. "Or somebody else with a bad conscience. Wait here."

I didn't linger to see whether he obeyed me. Just down the corridor from her room we had passed a window onto another fire escape on the same side of the building. I ran back to it and wrenched the window open in time to see Sonja, on the neighboring fire escape and one flight below me, heading for the ground. I didn't even think about what I was doing. I followed her. Behind me I could hear Nick kicking down her door; not very subtle, but at least he was direct.

FOURTEEN

SONJA WAS CLUMSIER than I was on the rickety fire stairs. I was pleased about that till I realized it was because she had a gun in one hand and I hadn't. I first became aware of the disparity when she shot at me. I was still half a floor above her and halfway across the building from her, with a lot of rusted metal framework between us, and I already knew her aim was poor, but that didn't stop me from making a brief and panicky effort to conceal myself behind the inch-wide railing bars while she went on scrambling down her set of stairs.

I'm pleased to report that I recovered my senses before she reached ground level, where she would have a really clear shot at me. That is, I recovered enough to move, but not enough to think of drawing Sharon's little .22. I'd like to say that I refrained for some logical reason, like maybe I needed both hands or I wanted to be sure to take her alive, but the plain fact is I forgot I was wearing it. I was accustomed to a weapon that had some weight to it. When I had my .38 with me, I knew I had it. Even accustomed as I was to carrying that extra weight around, I never forgot it was there. And now I was very aware that it wasn't there.

The rest of the way down, the race was for bigger stakes. I had either to find some sturdy concealment or get off the stairs before she did. Rusted iron fire escapes don't offer much sturdy concealment. It seemed obvious that she would reach the ground before me, and I'd be caught defenseless on the stairs.

There was no real reason to chase her. She didn't have anything I wanted except possibly some information that I could just as easily find elsewhere or get from her at a calmer time. When I reached a first story window I climbed through it.

When I got back up to her room I found Nick inside and was obscurely relieved to note that he had stopped short of breaking down the door, resorting instead, presumably, to a credit card or some other convenient piece of plastic to slip the lock. He was busily searching her belongings, and looked at me oddly when I came in. "She didn't kill you," he said.

"She tried. Find anything?"

His face had the set expression of a public performer in a crowd: the unseeing, unrevealing, impersonal mask of the politician, the actor, the stranger. His dark eyes were turned toward mine, but there was no hint of recognition, no sign that he was looking at another human being. He might have been staring blindly at a wall. "No. She got away?"

"Yes. What were you looking for?"

"I don't know." He bent over an open drawer of Sonja's clothing and picked up a neat stack of it without apparent interest or intention. His movements were curiously loose-jointed and jerky, like a puppet with tangled strings. "Where did she go?"

"I don't know." There was one chair in the room, a faded rattan construction that might once have been both attractive and comfortable. Now it looked unsanitary and possibly dangerous. I sat in it. "We'll find Lela, Nick."

It was, perhaps, the wrong thing to say. Certainly it did not have an exactly calming effect on him. All that pent-up energy burst free. The clothes he had been holding went flying. By the time they landed, the drawer he had taken them from was upended on the floor and Nick was on the opposite side of the room, his body braced against the bed-frame, slamming his fist against the cracked plaster wall. His eyes were closed, squeezed shut as if in an effort to shut out all the world at once. I remembered thinking, seemingly a long time ago, that his was the face of a man who could shed tears. That vulnerability was in evidence again. And with it, the fierce and deadly look of a trapped thing baring its teeth at its captors outside the bars of its cage.

"Jeez." His voice was a monotone of despair, punctuated by the dull, oddly shocking sound of his fist striking the wall. "Jesus, Jesus, Jesus." He opened his eyes and looked at me then, drawing back his fist as if to hit the wall again, and paused. For a long, frozen moment we remained like that: the wild-eyed Gypsy caught in an invisible cage, and the startled *gadjo* poised and helpless, watching him.

"You're always bleeding on other people's belongings." My voice sounded hollow in the silence after his outburst. I tried on a smile, knew it didn't fit, and waited.

He looked at the cracked plaster where his fist, bloodied by the impact of the first blow, had left a red impression each subsequent time he hit it. "Sorry," he said tonelessly.

"So don't hit it again."

His fist was still clenched on a level with his chest, poised to strike again. The knuckles were bruised and badly scraped, and he studied them with detached and clinical interest. "I got to find her," he said. "I got to find Lela. Before they hurt her again. She's just a kid, she don't deserve none of this, I got to find her!" His voice rose with the repetition, but starting as it did from a defeated and nearly inaudible monotone, it was not yet loud when he finished. Not loud, but it was deadly. He was at the limit of his endurance. If he found the enemy now, he would kill.

"We'll find her." I meant to soothe him, but my voice cracked. I cleared my throat. I did not know we would find her, and I was not sure I would lead him to her if we did. I had no desire to be responsible for a killing spree.

I needn't have worried. His baffled rage died as abruptly as it had begun. He blinked, and it was as if a light had gone out. His eyes went flat and featureless, his expression dead. "Sure." He glanced at his bloody knuckle-print on the wall and swiped at it absentmindedly with his elbow, smearing the red stains into the cracked plaster. "Sure."

"The wall doesn't matter, Nick. Leave it alone."

"Sure. Okay." He moved away from it, jerky and awkward again, and sat on the edge of the bed.

"You okay now?"

"I'm okay."

He wasn't, of course, but there was nothing else to say. I started poking through Sonja's belongings where he had left off, more because I needed something to do with my hands than because I expected to find anything useful. "Why d'you suppose Sonja ran from us?"

He shrugged, indifferent. "Because she is ashamed. Because she tried to kill me, you understand. She is ashamed of that."

"I wonder."

"What? You wonder what?"

"Whether Sonja would feel particularly ashamed of that. Somehow I doubt it. I bet she ran because she has the money you're after, and doesn't want to lose it."

"Was she carrying it?"

It was a valid point. She had not been carrying a hundred thousand dollars, not even if it was in thousand dollar bills. The purse she had been carrying was too small, and I would have noticed if it had been affixed to her person, even in pockets. "Okay, but I'll bet she knows where it is."

"She knows where Lela is, anyway."

"Why are you so sure of that?"

"She knows Lela's husband's family. She'd know where they are."

"Aren't there any other Gypsies around here? Surely there must be others you could ask about Lela."

"They won't talk to me. My father, he has told them lies. They don't trust me."

"Then help me look through her stuff. Maybe we'll find a bankbook or something."

"Gypsies don't put nothing in banks."

"Nick, for God's sake. Gypsies don't this, Gypsies don't that, you're always telling me what Gypsies do or don't do, and we're always finding out some of them do what they say they don't. Particularly the members of your family. Besides, a bankbook wouldn't be the only useful clue we could find. Come on. Look around. Hell, maybe we'll find the money.''

"If that's here, that money, Sonja wouldn't have left when she saw us. Anyway, I keep saying, if she has it, what was she looking for in your office and Sharon's place?''

Another valid point. "Never mind,'' I explained. "Come on, you don't know what we might find. Let's look.''

Sullenly, he pulled out the drawer of the bedside table to poke through its contents. I tried the top drawers in the bureau and came up with a business card from a travel agency that Nick had never heard of. He made me read aloud to him every word on the card, scowled at it in frustration when none of the information was useful, and went back to poking incuriously through the table drawer. I stuck the business card in my purse and returned to the bureau drawers. I found a lot of peasant blouses and lace underwear but no clues.

"This, what does this say?'' His voice was eager, his face animated again. He was holding up a matchbook with the jack of clubs printed on its cover.

"I don't know. Toss it over.'' I held out my hands, but he rose and hand carried the matchbook to me as though it were both precious and fragile.

"Here, look,'' he said. "On the back, there's an

address or something, here. See? What does it say?"

I read it to him. It was an address in the Mission District in San Francisco. "So what?"

"So that's maybe where we can find Lela." He was almost dancing with eagerness. "This on the front, this jack of clubs, it's the sign of her husband's mother's *ofisa*. The address, that will be where the *ofisa* is now."

"Unless it's an old matchbook."

I might not have spoken, for all the attention he paid me. "And where the *ofisa* is, there we might find Lela. Usually her husband's family, they all live in the same place as where she keeps her *ofisa*."

"Then we'll go see," I said.

"Oh, hell," he said. "Oh, damn." His face crumpled and he sat down suddenly on the bed as though his knees had given way. "Oh, *damn*."

"What? What is it?"

"The money," he said. "We ain't got the money to buy her back." He hurled the matchbook across the room and for a moment I thought we were in for another confrontation between his fist and the nearest wall, but he controlled himself with a visible effort and said in a tight, bitter voice, "It ain't no good. We can't get her."

"We've been over this before, Nick. They have no right to keep her if she doesn't want to stay."

"You don't understand." He stood up suddenly and then didn't go anywhere. He just stood there, every muscle in his body tensed for action he wouldn't take. "*Gajende!* You don't understand."

"I understand that families that beat little girls don't get to keep them, Nick. Bride-price or no bride-price. Hell, if it was their own kid they were beating, they couldn't keep her. It's against the law to beat people."

"Gypsies don't—"

I nearly hit him. "Don't *tell* me what Gypsies don't, damn you!" I studied him. "Are you really more interested in talking about the rules of Gypsy life than you are in rescuing your little sister from further abuse?"

He looked at me, beat and broken and confused, afraid to hope. "Ailie…"

"Because if you are, then you can just stand here and talk about it, but damned if I'll stand here and listen to you talk about it. You say she might be at this address. Okay. I'm gonna pick up Sharon and we're going to this address, and by God, if Lela's there, and if she wants to come away, then we'll get her away. And there won't be any damn discussion about bride-prices, or any other damn thing Gypsies do or don't do!"

To my utter and complete surprise, he grinned at me, a sweet, uncomplicated grin of pure delight. "You will, won't you?"

"Damn straight I will."

"It ain't right, you understand."

"Neither is beating people up."

"Maybe we better go get Sharon," he said.

FIFTEEN

THE SUN WAS almost directly overhead by the time we got back to Sharon. Her car must have felt like a sauna, even with the windows open. If I had been waiting in it as long as she had, I would have been looking sweaty, bedraggled, and miserable. She didn't look even slightly wilted. Her face was flushed with the heat, but instead of making her look hot and puffy, as it would me, it made her look rosy-cheeked and lively. She got out of the car when we parked behind her, moving with a dancer's casual grace, and I watched Nick sign over his soul to her again, as he had in the office. Men couldn't help it. They saw her in motion and all the blood rushed out of their brains to supply certain other portions of their anatomies. Standing still, she was a threat to every other living woman. In motion, she was a killer. And the worst of it was that she didn't mean it. Hell, she didn't even know it.

Fortunately I was never a really jealous person, at least not when Sharon was involved; I knew my limitations. But I got out of the car to meet her, so I wouldn't have to watch if Nick began to drool.

"Any sign of her here?" I leaned against my closed door and realized, when I heard the door slam on his side, that I had thereby momentarily blocked Nick's view of my partner Aphrodite. "She was at the hotel, but I lost her."

"She didn't come here. I take it you didn't talk to her?" She smiled a friendly greeting at Nick and leaned a hip against my car, her body turned so she could unobtrusively keep an eye on the *ofisa* while we talked.

"There wasn't time. As soon as Nick knocked, she started running." I told her about the chase, and she treated my part in it with the respect it deserved: she laughed at me.

"What did you think you'd do if you caught her?"

"It's not polite to laugh at your partner." Conscious of the contrast between us, I dusted my skirt with dustier hands and fussed uselessly with my hair, which was stuck in damp tendrils to my forehead and the back of my neck. "I already said I know it was stupid. The only smart thing we did was to search her room after she got away."

"That was smart? After all that gunfire, the area must've been crawling with cops. And you two pulled a B and E right under their noses."

"Not exactly under their noses. If there were any cops around, they were out in the alleys looking for whoever did the shooting, not in the hotel looking to see if someone was breaking into the room. Actually, I didn't see any cops around, anyway. They don't always investigate loud noises in neighborhoods like that, unless someone complains. They can't, or they wouldn't have time for anything else."

She shrugged. "Okay, what did you find in her room?"

"Well, nothing much, really." I pulled out the travel agency card. "This, and a matchbook Nick says belongs to Lela's husband's family business. There's an address on it. In the city."

She took the business card in one elegant hand and tapped it against the other. The jeweled nail glinted in the sun. "This is interesting. S'pose Nancy/Sonja is planning a trip somewhere?"

I put my own hands behind my back, where I wouldn't notice the dirt and the broken nails. "I'd bet on it."

"Let's find out where."

"Why?"

"Curiosity. Also, the farther she's going, the more likely it is that she has the *hukkaben* money, right?"

"Right, I suppose, but so what? The money's hers if it's anyone's. It was she who stole it, after all."

"And that makes it hers?"

"Well, it sure isn't ours."

"I'd still like to keep my eye on it."

"Part of that's mine," said Nick. "I helped with the *hukkaben*. I should get my share." He said it belligerently, but he had a hard time meeting her eyes. Men often had a hard time speaking up to her at all. It was one of the few disadvantages to such beauty. I always wondered how she could ever have a sensible conversation with a man when one look at her deprived his brain of oxygen.

"Right," said Sharon. She had no idea what it might have cost him to make that assertion in the face of her own obvious and innocent greed. "Let's see where she's traveling."

"We were talking about going to San Francisco," I said. "Nick thinks Lela might be at the address on this matchbook cover."

She nodded agreeably. "We'll do that next. After we check with the travel agency."

I gave in gracefully. "How do you want to handle that? Phone, or in person?"

She glanced at the address again. "It's not far from here. Let's try it in person."

We left her car where it was, for the time being, and took mine to the travel agency. It was in a block of renovated shops with cute names like Wholly Cow, which ought to have been a butcher shop but was in fact a restaurant, and Trendy Wendy's, which seemed to be a fashion boutique. The travel agency struck a more sober note with

Tuttle Travel painted in sedate block letters on the gleaming plate-glass window. The display area to the left of the doorway contained carefully fanned travel brochures on the window seat and a model plane suspended by nylon fishing line above them so that it looked like it was about to take a nosedive onto the beautifully photographed beaches of the unidentified ocean that graced the front of the center brochure. The window display to the right of the door held a model train track with a three-car model train endlessly circling a blue glass lake set in a field of grayish powder that may have been meant to resemble snow.

We found a parking place on the same block, fed the meter, and argued briefly over how many of us would go inside. Sharon and I thought Nick should wait in the car. Nick disagreed. The three of us trooped inside together without any kind of plan as to how to extract the information we wanted.

As it happened, we didn't need a plan: the travel agent was a middle-aged heterosexual male. I don't think he even noticed that Sharon had Nick and me in tow. He never once looked at either of us. When we opened the door, he looked up from his computer at Sharon in the lead, and I could see his brain turn to Jell-O Pudding on the spot. It was a no-blame situation: she didn't do it on purpose, and men couldn't help how they reacted. It wasn't an invariable result of confronting an unsuspecting man with Sharon's appearance, but it could be very useful when it did happen, and it happened often enough that I had learned to count on it. Sharon didn't. She just thought there were a disproportionate number of men in the world with shaky knees, minor speech impediments, and low IQs.

Sharon didn't even bother to lie to this guy. She just told him Nick's sister had made travel arrangements through his agency and we wanted to check on her itinerary. He punched it up on his computer without a moment's hesitation and nearly tripped over his desk in his effort to make sure she was comfortable while she read the screen. Maybe travel agents always hand out information that freely; I don't really know, having seldom had occasion to request it. I'd like to think that if I make travel plans through an agency they might not be as readily revealed to random strangers as Nancy/Sonja's were, but this didn't seem to be the time to mention that.

Sonja and an unnamed companion were booked on a flight to Europe and across it with several tourist stops on the way. The tickets were paid for in cash before MacMurray was killed, which meant we still didn't know for sure whether she had the *hukkaben* money, but at least we could guess that she had been in possession of it at some time in the past. Whether she had subsequently given it to MacMurray was anybody's guess at this point.

Sharon broke the travel agent's heart by telling him good-bye, and we returned to my car with new information, if not much wiser. "It don't really matter who's got the money," said Nick. "I got to get Lela away from that family, that's all."

The street seemed even hotter after our brief stay in the air-conditioned comfort of the travel agent's office. Sharon opened the door for Nick to get in the back seat while I put the rotor arm in the engine. I broke another fingernail doing it, and got grease on the front of my dress when I closed the hood. Some days are like that.

When we were all three in the car again, Sharon settled in comfortably as though preparing for a long stay and said with innocent cruelty, "That fellow didn't seem very bright. How do you suppose he manages to run a complicated business like that?"

She was perfectly serious. She was an intelligent woman, perceptive about a lot of things, but totally blind to the effect she had on the average man. Sometimes I found that endearing, sometimes irritating: this time I found it irritating. "Don't be stupid." I put one finger in my mouth to chew on the broken nail. It tasted of motor oil. "He's probably brilliant when you're not around."

"What do you mean?" She turned in her seat to scowl at me. It should have made her look ugly. It didn't. "Oh, you mean he was bowled over by my stunning beauty. Come on, Ailie, what's the matter with you? Sure, I'm pretty, but not any prettier than you, for instance, and you never claim your great beauty knocks guys over." She turned frontward again, kicked off her shoes, and put her feet on the dash.

"She should," Nick said, surprising both of us. "It does."

"What?" I twisted in my seat to stare at him, convinced I must have misheard. "What are you talking about?"

He met my gaze. "I said, it does. Your great beauty. It does what she said. It knocks guys over."

I faced front abruptly. "Don't be silly, Nick. It's sweet of you to say that, but—"

"Are you serious? You didn't know that? Jeez, the two of you, you're like movie stars or something, and neither of you knows it?"

We both blushed. "Um," said Sharon.

"This is great," I said, "but, um..." I dropped the car keys on the floor and had to bend under the steering wheel to find them.

"It's not getting us anywhere," Sharon said decisively.

Nick grinned at us, enjoying himself. "You're embarrassed!"

"Well," I said, fumbling with the keys and nearly dropping them again. I don't know why I had gone quite so clumsy. It was not as though I had never been complimented before.

"I think we should have a plan," said Sharon.

Nick was delighted. "I always thought beautiful women, especially *gadje*, they was always stuck-up about it, and they used it, you know, to get what they wanted or whatever. And look at you, the two of you—"

"A plan," said Sharon.

"And you don't even know," said Nick.

"That's enough, Nick." I said it rather more sharply than I meant to.

He subsided, grinning.

"What sort of plan?" I put the key in the ignition, ready to implement a plan.

"I don't know," said Sharon. "I'm still bothered by that money. What the hell was Nancy looking for in the office and in my apartment, if she already has it? But if she doesn't have it, where is it?"

"When I searched Ailie's house," said Nick, "I was looking for the money because Sonja told me it was there."

"But we know it wasn't." I was getting a headache from staring out at the sundrenched street with its border of glittering cars and blinding windows. I closed my eyes and rubbed the back of one hand hard against my forehead, then remembered how dirty my hands were and craned to see my reflection in the rearview mirror, to see whether I'd transferred motor oil or rust stains onto my forehead.

"If we could find it, we could use it to buy Lela back," said Nick.

"We'll get her back without it." My forehead seemed relatively clean. I leaned my head back against the hot plastic headrest.

"It's just a piece of the puzzle that doesn't fit anywhere," said Sharon. She had her head back, too, and her feet crossed on the dash, and I wondered whether she felt as comfortable as she looked.

"What is?" said Nick.

"Her searching the office and my apartment," said Sharon. "I don't like pieces of puzzles that don't fit."

"It don't matter," said Nick. "I just want to get Lela." With my head back, I could see his reflection in the rearview mirror. His brown eyes were shadowed almost to black, and the whites of them glinted in the light.

"It matters," I said. "There are still two murders to solve, either or both of which may very probably be connected in some way to that money."

"I still got to get Lela," said Nick.

"I thought you'd decided Sonja committed both murders," said Sharon.

"She was present when we found Nick's Auntie

Tia," I said. "And she has a .38, which is what killed MacMurray."

"You have a .38," said Sharon.

"Had," I said. "The cops have it now. But your point is well taken. Ownership of a .38 is not proof of guilt."

"Auntie Tia was killed with a knife," said Nick.

"Your knife, according to Sonja," I said.

"My father Django, he likes knives," Nick said thoughtfully.

"Your father Django," said Sharon. "This is the man who beat his son bloody, and sold his baby daughter into slavery?"

"Not slavery," said Nick, offended. "I keep saying, it's not wrong, the way we marry. The bride-price. It's only that my father let that boy have her, who is not so good for her and whose family is not good for her."

"Understatement," said Sharon.

"What?" said Nick.

"She means you're right, getting beat up is not good for a person," I said.

"Oh. Yes," said Nick. "That's why it would be okay to give them back only half the bride-price."

"That's why it will be okay to give them back none of the bride-price," I said.

"Why would your father have killed your Auntie Tia?" asked Sharon. "I mean okay, he sounds like a pretty unpleasant guy, but does he go around killing people a lot?''

"No," said Nick. "Of course not. I don't know why he would kill Auntie Tia. I only know he likes knives, that's all."

"Has he killed somebody before, with a knife? Is that why you say that?''

"I told you, Gypsies don't kill people."

"But someone killed Auntie Tia," she said. "And it might have been your father."

"It *might* have been." He scowled at her.

"Why would he?"

"I don't know."

Something in his tone triggered a half-buried memory. I turned to look at him. "Is that how you got that scar on your arm?" He was shaking his head in a desperate, defiant negative before I finished the question. "Did your father do that to you?''

"My father, he don't..." He met my gaze and let his voice trail into silence. He had said he wouldn't lie to me. "Damn you," he said instead.

Sharon took her feet down and turned to stare at him. "I saw that scar. On your forearm, right here." She indicated the outside of her own forearm, the area most exposed when one held a bent arm up to defend one's face or body. "Is that what happened? Did your father attack you with a knife? His own son?''

Nick put his arm down out of sight beside him. "So what?" His tone was sullen, his gaze fierce.

"So this is a really unpleasant man we're talking about," said Sharon. She turned around, put her feet up, and relaxed in her seat again.

"I told you that already." He looked out the window, affecting boredom. "Are we going to sit here all day, or what? It's hot, you know." He said it as though we might not otherwise have noticed. "If we're not going to go get Lela, what I'd like is, I could use a cold beer."

Sharon smiled thoughtfully to herself. "It is hot," she said.

"You're right," I said.

"We're not much further along, are we?" she said. "We know Sonja had enough money for airline tickets. We know this Django person likes knives. And we know that a lot of people own .38 caliber handguns."

"We know the address of Lela's husband's mother's *ofisa*," I said.

"True," said Sharon. "And we know that Nick would like a cold beer."

"Come to that, so would I," I said.

"Good, that's settled," said Sharon. "We'll get lunch, complete with cold beers, and then we'll go to the city to see what we can see. It is lunchtime, isn't it?"

She had at last found something on which all three of us could agree.

SIXTEEN

WE DIDN'T TALK much business during lunch, but when we left the restaurant we were agreed that the next move was to drive to San Francisco to steal Lela from her husband's family. We could worry later about the money and the murders. Getting that little girl away from a family that abused her became more pressing the more I thought about it, and even Nick was ready to agree that since we didn't have half the bride-price, it made sense to try to get her without it. He could always pay the family later if he really felt it was necessary.

We took both cars out of Oakland and left Sharon's at her apartment building. It would have been quicker to leave for the city from Oakland, but Sharon was as fond of her car as I was of my Capri, and it wasn't a wise plan to leave a cherished car undefended in Oakland. Nick very politely got out and moved to the back seat when Sharon got in.

There were people out in their boats again, white sails gleaming against the dark of the water. The Richmond-San Rafael bridge, usually obscured by distance and smog, arced cleanly over the north bay, startlingly visible in the wind-scoured heat. The bright orange of the Golden Gate Bridge made it look oddly defiant against the blue ocean and the luminous sky. Nothing looked quite real; it was as though we were watching a Chamber of Commerce film about these places. Even the steel and concrete towers of the city looked like faerie palaces in the heat-shimmered distance. The islands in the bay were green and golden jewels, tantalizing little pockets of potential myth and magic where the deer might share space with unicorns and elves.

Traffic on the Bay Bridge was minimal at that time of day. We stopped to pay the toll—San Francisco is like a circus; you have to pay to get in but it's free to come out—and didn't have to jockey for position beyond the toll booths; all the lanes were clear. We had all the Capri's windows open. Once we got going again, conversation would have been difficult over the roar of the wind. None of us tried it; there was nothing to say. Wind whipped through the car, hot and stinking of distant grass fires.

Sharon would probably have liked a more detailed plan than we had, but there was no way we could make one when all we had were an address and a hope. She spent the time on the bridge staring out across the bay with thoughtful eyes, as though she'd never seen it before. The Bay Area does that to a person, starting out beautiful and changing faces with every change of weather and light, so that even after a lifetime of staring at its sheltering hills and sunstruck waters, no view of it becomes boring or routine.

Nick spent the bridge time staring out the window too, but from what I could see of him in the rearview mirror I didn't think he was enjoying the view. His eyes had gone dark and wild again, his face dangerous. I thought he was miles away from us, but when we got off the freeway and conversation again became possible, it was he who spoke first.

"When he wanted to hit somebody, I always got in his way," he said. "Girls you don't hit. They're the money makers. They're special. I would get between him and Lela so the belt or the fists, they would not hit her. Even when I was little and she was just a baby, I knew to do that. She never had to get beat up if I was there."

I glanced at him in the rearview mirror. There was no need to ask who he was talking about. "It's okay, Nick. You'll be there for her real soon."

He might not have heard me. "I used to pretend I was more afraid than I was, so he'd know I was mocking him, and he'd think I wasn't afraid at all. Then he'd get mad at me for real, and forget about her." He fell silent, the near-black of his eyes glittering like polished onyx. After a moment he shook his head briefly, a gesture of bewildered irritation.

"She don't know what to do. She ain't got no experience. It ain't right to hit girls."

"It ain't right to hit anybody," said Sharon.

"Usually," I said.

She glanced at me. "Okay, usually."

Nick wasn't listening. "I should've been there. Maybe I could've stopped him selling her to that boy. I know the family. They ain't no good, that family. Maybe I could've stopped this thing."

"We'll stop it now, Nick," I said.

He fell silent again, brooding, his wild eyes gazing sightlessly out at the sun-drenched city streets. I wanted to say something more, something that would ease the grim line of his mouth and soothe away the pain that tilted his eyebrows and drew two deep vertical lines between them, but there was nothing to say.

I drove up the hill into the Mission District, turned on Twenty-First, and started looking for the address.

It wasn't far. I missed the number but recognized the signs in the windows; it was another *ofisa* like the one in Oakland, complete with exotic curtains and oversized playing cards on the glass door. The building itself was one of those pink stucco apartment buildings so common to the area, square and sedate with chintz curtains in most of the windows and decorative ceramic tile around the door frame.

The *ofisa* was a storefront on the ground floor, where once there had been a parking garage.

"There! That's it!" Nick's voice was sharp. "And look, there is my father's car. The Buick, that's his. Stop the car!"

"Not in the middle of the street, Nick." I meant to sound soothing, but it came out more like irritated. "Give me a chance to find a parking spot, okay?" The street was nearly deserted in the heat of the day, but the parking spaces that lined it were nearly all occupied. Gleaming black Chevy lowriders pressed their shining chrome bumpers aggressively against dusty little Audis and Hondas and crumpled Fords.

"Up there, there's a spot, take that one." Nick gestured wildly, arms flailing, his voice tight with anxiety and excitement. "Hurry, somebody else will get it, we got to stop here, we got to get inside, I'll kill that bastard, stop the car!"

The parking place he pointed out was far enough from the *ofisa* that we would not be visible to anyone inside. Nick could barely sit still; the beleaguered patience with which he had forcefully held himself still all the way across the bay was clearly worn through now. If the Capri had been a fourdoor, he would have been out and running before I brought it to a stop. As it was, he fussed and fumed as though I were taking all day, even though I was rather proud of my parallel parking and managed to get it this time in one smooth move. He started pounding on the back of Sharon's seat before she had her seat belt released.

"Have patience," she said. "You'll live longer."

"Out, get out, I gotta." He seemed to be losing command of the English language. "He's here, do you see he is here? I gotta, I want to, my sister Lela needs me."

"Okay, Nick, okay," I said. Sharon had got out by then, and if I hadn't been looking her way instead of getting out myself, we would have been in trouble. Nick surged out the door behind her, and somehow managed to snag my purse on his way. "Hey!" I grabbed the purse straps. "What the hell?" I yanked at the purse with one desperate hand, pulling him off balance before he could get all the way out the door.

Sharon must have figured it out before I did. She struck his shoulder hard with the heel of her hand so that he fell back into the back seat, then followed through by shoving the front seat back into place and sitting down herself, effectively blocking him from exit. She looked at me. "Your gun's in there, right?"

I probably looked as stunned as I felt. Not only had I more or less forgotten the thing was there, but I would not have guessed that Nick seriously wanted to use it on his father. "Yeah. The .22. He saw me take off the holster and stow the gun in my purse while we were waiting for you to park your car in Berkeley.'' I felt apologetic, as if I were the one who had made the wrong move. ''The holster's uncomfortable for a long drive.''

''I'll kill him.'' Nick wasn't tracking very well. He was drunk on rage and bad memories that he had been cultivating all the way across the bridge. ''Gimme that. I'm gonna kill the son of a bitch.''

''Nick.'' I tugged at the purse, but he wouldn't let go. He couldn't get it open and couldn't get it from me, but he hadn't figured that out yet. ''Nick.''

''I shoulda been there for her.'' He clutched at the purse with both hands, blindly.

''Nick, stop it.'' He tugged. I tugged back. ''I won't let you have it. You're not going to kill your father. Come on, calm down. We'll get Lela, but not that way.''

''Let me go.'' He scowled at me.

''Let go of the purse.'' I scowled at him.

''Stop that.'' Sharon scowled at both of us. ''Something's happening.''

''I know,'' I said. ''It's called mutiny.''

''No, look.'' She gestured behind us, toward the *ofisa*. ''That's Nancy. Sonja. Who's the other one?''

Nick let go of the purse so suddenly I nearly fell over, and turned clear around in his seat to stare out the back window. "Lela!" Turning again, he lurched toward the door, but Sharon stopped him.

"Hold it," she said. "Just be calm."

"I gotta get out," he said.

"What are they doing?" I said. My view was obstructed by Nick's antics.

"Going toward a car," said Sharon.

Nick twisted around to look out the window again. "Django's car," he said, his voice rising. "They're getting in Django's car. They'll get away. Let me out, I gotta go to her. That's my little sister. She needs me."

I leaned against my door, peering out the back window, and managed to get a look at Sonja and Lela as they approached Django's car. Sonja looked much the same as she had in Oakland, though less dangerous without a .38 in hand. Lela looked more like eight than thirteen. She was a tiny little thing with silky black hair that hung to her waist and sheltered her face from my view. She was dressed in the same kind of full skirt and peasant blouse as Sonja, without the shawl or the kerchief on her head.

Nick had been watching, too. At the sight of that small figure he hurled himself at Sharon's seat-back again, making inarticulate sounds in his throat. Sharon ignored him. She had settled comfortably in her seat with the side mirror adjusted so she could watch Sonja and Lela in it without turning.

I couldn't tell whether Lela went willingly or not. Sonja had a firm grip on her upper arm and herded her toward the car with urgent determination, all the while throwing anxious glances back over her shoulder at the *ofisa* door. Lela opened the car door for herself and got in docilely enough, but maybe she was just too cowed to make any objection no matter what people asked of her. Sonja slammed the door behind her and ran around to the driver's side.

Nick hurled himself at Sharon's seat again. "Lela!" His voice was almost a howl that broke when he hit the seat. The force of his attack bounced Sharon forward, but she caught herself with one hand on the dash, braced her feet, and leaned back again without a word to watch the scene in her side mirror. Nick uttered a string of Romany curses and subsided, scowling bitterly, muttering to himself. "You gotta let me out, I gotta go to her, God knows what Sonja's doing. I gotta help Lela, *damn* it let me out of here!" He managed to sound quite fierce at the end of that.

"Wait," said Sharon. She was cool and calm and totally in control of the situation.

Nick lurched forward and tried to crawl between the two seats. I shoved him back, still watching past him out the back window. Sonja started Django's car and ground the gears so badly it was audible from where we were parked. I started the Capri again, but before I got it in gear the *ofisa* door crashed open and a huge man, barrel-shaped and greasy-haired, emerged scowling into the sunlight.

He must have weighed three hundred pounds. His skin was like wheat-bread dough, plump and freckled. His cheeks were round and dark with the stubble of a beard, and his bulging eyes stared out from under bushy black brows in fierce and deadly rage. Open-mouthed, arms akimbo, eyes burning, he stood poised for a long moment in the killing sun and stared after his daughters like an avenging demon from some foul and violent mythology, intent on destruction. The fabric of his shirt was stained and wrinkled, dark in the armpits and down the front of his massive chest. His trousers looked like Salvation Army rejects, baggy at the knees and seat, hung from his hips by a cracked leather belt that threatened to give way at any moment under the strain. Only his boots, thick-soled and shiny with polish, looked new and well cared for.

At the sight of him, Nick cowered instinctively, curling himself into a tight little ball in one corner of the back seat, his arms half-lifted as if to defend his head. I felt a tendency to cower myself and had to resist the impulse to crouch down in my seat in an effort to become invisible.

"That must be Django?" said Sharon. She had to raise her voice to be heard over the squealing tires of the fleeing Buick as Sonja peeled out of her parking space and into the traffic lane. She never looked back. I watched her. Once safely on her way she slowed and proceeded to the end of the block at a sedate pace, without a glance in her rearview mirror. The possibility of being followed must simply not have occurred to her.

Nick was watching the man behind us. "Yeah, Django." His voice was hoarse. "That, he's my father."

Django, seeing his own car drive down Twenty-First Street past us and away from him, lurched massively across the sidewalk to a parked Lincoln, wrenched the door open, and somehow managed to wedge his bulk in under the steering wheel. I put the Capri in gear. Django started the Lincoln and pulled skillfully away from the curb. Angry as he was, he didn't lay any rubber. For some reason, that unnerved me. I had seen his face. His driving was too calm, too precise, to match that enraged scowl. It made him seem even more deadly; it turned the rage from an honest human emotion to the cold calculation of a killer.

I waited till the Lincoln had passed us, then pulled out and fell in behind it. I had been clutching the steering wheel so tightly that my fingers hurt. I found myself cringing at the threat of his notice, but like his daughter, he never once looked back.

SEVENTEEN

A HIGH SPEED three-car chase through San Francisco traffic was not my idea of a fun way to spend the afternoon. Fortunately, Sonja remained blithely unaware of the minor parade behind her and Django didn't push her. Having nearly run two cars onto the sidewalk in his effort to get directly behind her when we turned off Twenty-First onto Mission Street, he seemed content to stay there, and he remained blithely unaware of my car behind his.

I didn't have to endanger any other drivers to get directly behind him; he cleared space enough for both of us when he made the turn. We proceeded up and down the hills of San Francisco in a happy little row for quite a while before anything happened to disturb the status quo. Traffic was heavier now that the full heat of the day had settled in over the city. People who might have walked on their various errands on a cooler day, in fog or even in rain, retreated to the air-conditioned sanctuary of their automobiles under the unaccustomed glare of this alien sun. Except for minor crises at a couple of stoplights, our three cars were unaffected by those around us.

Whenever I caught a glimpse of Lela and Sonja in the Buick in front of Django's Lincoln, they seemed to be involved in animated conversation. My guess was they were trying to decide where to go or what to do next. We were near a freeway entrance way the hell across town when they apparently reached a decision and got into the freeway entrance lane. Unfortunately, Django didn't seem to like that idea. When they got into the entrance lane he speeded up and edged them right back out of it.

Sonja almost lost it, right there. She'd had no idea her father was behind her till he came roaring up to push her out of her chosen lane and into another that was already occupied. Between the shock of seeing him and the difficulty of making a place for herself in the new lane, she lost control of the Buick long enough to sideswipe an innocent Nissan that wasn't quite quick enough in its effort to get out of her way. She recovered neatly, and the Nissan wasn't much damaged. Its driver threw fits when he realized she wasn't stopping, but I didn't have time to worry about his problems. Django was pushing the pace now, herding Sonja away from the freeway entrance; and she, now that she was aware of his presence, was in even more of a hurry than he was. It was all I could do to keep up with them without sideswiping somebody myself.

We passed the freeway entrance ramp at speed,

going downhill and coming up too fast on a crimson stoplight. Sonja swerved into the oncoming lane and went right through the light. Django hesitated, brake lights flashing, then made up his mind and charged through after her, horn blaring to warn oncoming traffic. He was too close behind Sonja; cars on the cross street were still sliding out of control from their effort to dodge her. One of them fishtailed right into Django's bumper, but they didn't lock, and it was a little Toyota against that whacking great Lincoln, so he may never even have noticed he was hit. The Toyota stopped where it was, smack in the middle of the intersection. In order to go through behind Django, I had to pull around it. At least the light was green by then.

Sonja crossed two lanes of traffic to take the next left, headed back west toward Golden Gate Park. Django followed in her wake, leaving stalled cars fuming behind them both. That made it relatively easy for me on that turn; the obstructing traffic wasn't moving.

I was beginning to wonder where the police were. SFPD was usually right on top of things. But I had never before been part of a high-speed chase through the city streets. Maybe that sort of thing didn't alarm them as much as it did me. I'm a good driver, but last in line is a bad position. I had to thread my way through whatever mess Sonja and Django made, and sometimes they made quite a mess. Sonja took to the sidewalks once to avoid oncoming traffic on a one-way street. Django followed without hesitation, and the two of them rammed rubbish cans and parking meters and anything else that got in their way, throwing debris out into the traffic lanes. Fortunately, nothing living got in their way.

The scattered debris stopped oncoming cars so I could stick to the street, but I had trouble with some of the trash cans. I couldn't dodge them and the cars both. My Capri lost a headlight and gained a nasty scratch along one side from a rolling Dumpster. I suppose I should have been grateful that was the only damage we sustained, but at the time I wasn't thinking that clearly.

They came off the sidewalk at the end of that block, and in the middle of the next block Sonja turned right across Django's path to take an alleyway on the other side of the street. He skidded past the alley, fishtailed into a line of parking meters, and came almost to a full stop before he got going again, facing the alley so he could pull in after Sonja. I had to decide whether to try to stop and wait for him to lead the chase after Sonja, or lead him into the alley, which would reveal my interest in the chase. I led him. If neither of them had noticed my existence by now, they were terminally unobservant and wouldn't notice no matter what I did. Windowless brick walls flashed by on either side as we skated through the turn and accelerated down the shadowed alley, straddling a runnel of oily water that trickled along the center of the cracked concrete.

Django noticed us, all right. When he got going again he entered the alleyway behind us at greater speed than I would have thought that Lincoln could do in the distance he had, and rammed the back of my Capri so hard he nearly shoved us right up against the parked cars that lined one side of our way. I spun the wheel and stomped on the gas, gaining us just enough space to save our lives till we reached the end of the alley. I had to slow there for oncoming traffic. Django crashed up against us again in an apparent effort to go right through us to reach the alley across the street where the Buick's taillights were visible as Sonja hit the brakes at the end of the next block.

Sharon yelled something, but I didn't hear what it was. I was concentrating on getting out of Django's way. He scraped past us with a wrenching screech of metal on metal and roared after Sonja. She signaled a turn. I took the chance that it was good driving habits, not a deliberate effort to mislead her followers, and spun my wheel in that direction. Fortunately the street onto which we emerged was one-way in the direction I wanted, so I didn't have to contend with oncoming traffic. I took another chance at the next corner: I turned in the direction we had been going. If Sonja had doubled back on her path I would have lost them both. She didn't. She careened across the street I was on and kept going, with Django hard on her tail. I reached the corner in time to slide neatly in behind them. My poor Capri, battered as it had become in the last few minutes, still handled beautifully. I was actually beginning to enjoy myself.

The three of us were headed west again in a neat little row, past the close-packed Victorian houses of the Haight-Ashbury district on one side and the cool green panhandle of Golden Gate Park on the other. Afternoon sun glinted on the glass and metalwork of parked cars flashing by on both sides of the street and cast a leaf-patterned filigree of gold under the trees.

"Jeez," said Nick.

"My sentiments exactly," said Sharon.

"Where the hell is she leading us?" I said.

"Where the hell are the cops when you want one?" asked Sharon. "If we didn't want them, they'd have stopped us miles ago."

"Since they haven't come to us," I said, "I wonder why Sonja doesn't take us to them? If she's afraid of Django, that would be the logical move."

"To go to the cops?" said Nick. "No, jeez, you don't go to the cops."

"Why not?" asked Sharon.

"Because you don't," said Nick. "Sonja, she

wouldn't even think of that, of going to the cops. Look out!''

The warning was directed at me, because we were coming up on another clogged intersection and Sonja had just run the yellow light. ''We'll make it,'' I said. Both Django and I stepped on the gas and I hit my horn. We didn't make it on the yellow, but we made it.

Sharon took a deep breath and tried to look calm. ''The police wouldn't let your father hurt your sister,'' she said. ''They can't hope to get away from him this way. More likely we'll all be killed. You really think going to the cops would be worse than dying?''

''What you maybe don't understand,'' said Nick, ''is that Gypsies don't do nothing like that. Go to the cops. That, we don't never do. The cops, they're *gajende*. We don't need no *gajende* cops to solve our problems.''

Sonja had given up on evasive tactics and was headed straight for the park. Maybe she thought she could outrun him there, on the relatively empty park roadways. If she'd asked, I could have told her that wouldn't work. The roadways wouldn't be all that empty. But she didn't ask.

''Besides,'' said Nick, ''those cars, they're probably stolen.''

''What cars?'' asked Sharon, confused.

''The ones my sister and my father are driving.''

"Oh," said Sharon. "Great."

"What I don't understand…," said Nick.

When he didn't finish the sentence, I prodded him. "What don't you understand?"

"This running," he said thoughtfully.

Sharon turned in her seat to look at him, thought better of it, and turned to face front again, clinging to her seat belt's shoulder strap. "You don't understand why they're running? I thought it was obvious. That man looks like he'll kill them the minute he catches them."

"That I don't understand, too," said Nick.

"You don't understand what? Why he'd kill them?" I asked. "I thought you told us he was an evil man who'd kill just about anybody on whim."

"Not like that, what you said, I didn't say that." He was impatient with me. "He is evil, yes, my father, but he is Gypsy, too. He still lives the life. Even when he is breaking the rules of our ways, you understand, he does not think in the ways of *gajende*. You understand?"

"No," I said.

"People such as yourself," he said, and hesitated. "*Gadje*," he said, and thought about that. "What it is, people who are not Gypsies, who are not raised in the life, in our ways, they think different from us. They steal from each other."

"Gypsies don't steal?" said Sharon.

"Not from each other," said Nick.

"We've been through this before," I said. "He's chasing his sister because she stole from his family, but Gypsies don't steal."

"And we don't kill," said Nick, untroubled by sarcasm. "But *gajende,* they are crazy. They might kill and steal and rape, they might do anything. You cannot tell what they might do. They have no rules."

"They might sell their daughters to families that beat them, you mean?" asked Sharon.

Nick ignored her. "What I don't understand, why is my father so angry? Why would he kill my sisters?"

The entrance to the park whipped past us and fell behind. There were green shadows on both sides now, and the road curved gently between its rows of parked cars baking in the sun.

"Maybe Sonja took Lela without paying back half the bride-price, just like we were going to do," said Sharon.

"Sonja, she would never do that." He sounded quite certain. "That is not our way."

"You were going to do it," said Sharon.

"That's different," said Nick.

"If Sonja didn't do that, does that mean she paid?" I said. "Because if she paid, where did she get the money? Do you s'pose she and Lela have the *hukkaben* money with them? Now?"

"Look out, that car," said Nick.

"I see it," I said.

"Don't worry, she's a good driver," said Sharon. She didn't sound altogether convinced.

"They're getting away," said Nick.

We were deep in the park by now, and the roads were emptier than the city streets, but not by much. I kept having to dodge people pulling out of parking places, and once I nearly collided with an oncoming car in an effort to avoid a soccer ball that came hurtling out from between parked cars in front of me. "They're not getting away," I said. "They took that turn up there. I know that road. It turns into a dirt track that dead-ends by the swan pond about half a mile into the forest." I took the turn onto the new road too fast and skidded into the oncoming lane, but this road really was deserted, so we were okay. "This is it. She's cornered herself. If she follows this to the end she won't even be able to turn around to get out of here."

"Stay with them," said Sharon.

"Right." If we were along when they reached the end of the road, maybe Django would think twice about hurting those girls. Having seen his face, and having heard Nick's stories, I doubted it, but if all else failed, I had Sharon's spare .22 in my purse, and I knew she was carrying hers in her purse. Between us, we ought to be able to stop him.

The forest closed in on us; we were plunging now through swimming shadows under gathering trees. The paved road turned into a gravel track, then a dirt path. Eucalyptus trees leaned their resinous branches down over us, brushing the car roof. Wild lupin thrust purple blossoms through patches of fallen leaves. The forest floor was neatly manicured here, as it was everywhere in the park; the grass was as smooth as a golf course and all the underbrush was intentional and trimmed; but the resultant neatness did nothing to detract from the feeling of being in a primeval forest far from civilization. It added to that impression by providing empty space and a sense of isolation. There might have been no living soul but us for miles around.

The dirt path was pitted and rocky, forcing all three cars to slow almost to a crawl, but Sonja kept going. Maybe she thought the road would widen out again, turn paved, and lead us back to civilization. The hot summer air pressed in through the open windows, heavy with the rich scents of smog, eucalyptus, and cut grass. We crept up a slight rise under spreading broadleafed trees I didn't recognize, passed through a saffron drift of sour oxalis that swept across the path into the shade of a bank of pink oleander, and burst onto a sunny expanse of clover-dotted meadow before the path started down again on the other side of the rise.

The swan pond was ahead of us, a serene forest pool on which white swans floated, their long-necked reflections rippling on the glassy surface.

The hillside beyond the water was white with a sweet cascade of waxy flowers. There were crimson, rambling roses climbing a mossy wooden fence, and drifts of tiny bells in the shade at their feet, strange, frail shapes of white and yellow and germander blue. The hillside down to the pond, less well-tended than the rest of the forest, harbored sunny patches of bright orange poppies, yellow mustard, and even lavender, pungent and sweet like an opened jar of potpourri in the summer air. I wanted to live forever. Or at least until tomorrow.

At that moment, it seemed unlikely that I would.

EIGHTEEN

THE BUICK RUSHED down the slope to the end of the path and skidded to a stop in sun-dappled shadows between the pond and a steep bank of brilliant yellow oxalis and tangled morning glories, their white-centered trumpets still open in the wooded shade. Aware she was trapped, Sonja tried to slam the Buick into reverse while she was still moving, a panic maneuver that killed the engine and ground the gears audibly even over the roar of the Lincoln wallowing down the slope behind her like a tank.

Django hit the brakes when he was halfway down and crimped the wheel so that he slid sideways the rest of the way, tires ripping into the parched grass beside the path, bumpers tearing branches from oleanders and rhododendrons along the way. He judged it to perfection: the Lincoln came to rest at an angle across the path no more than five feet from the back bumper of the Buick, which had slid off the path till its front tires rested several inches deep in mud and water. Even if Sonja got the engine started again, and could work her way out of the gluey edge of the pond, Django had effectively blocked any chance she had of escaping.

I had fallen behind on the way up the slope. Sonja and Lela were out of the Buick before we crested the rise and turned down toward the pond. They both got out on the driver's side, the side farthest from Django, and started up the saffron-carpeted bank toward the gloomy shadows of the sheltering forest, dragging a heavy suitcase between them. Nick shouted something inarticulate and tried to get the Capri's back window open. It was the kind of window that doesn't roll down, but only pops outward an inch or two. He wasn't satisfied with an inch or two. I didn't know which would give first, the glue that held the window to its hinge, or his fist. There wasn't time to worry about it; we came over the hill too fast, and I had all I could do to keep control of the Capri while we bounced down the slope.

Django was half in and half out of the car, aiming a .38 through the window at his daughters, who were making little headway up the bank, lugging the heavy suitcase between them. They kept slipping on crushed oxalis and tripping on vines, falling on the suitcase and each other, scrambling to their feet, scarlet and turquoise peasant skirts flying, screaming curses both in Romany and in English, and cringing every time Django shot at them, but making no real effort to get out of the line of fire.

Fortunately, Django was as bad a shot as his daughter. He looked so angry, he probably couldn't see straight. He too, was screaming curses in both Romany and English, and I was glad I couldn't understand the ones in Romany; the ones in English were bad enough. The angle from which we were approaching was such that I had a clear three-quarters view of his face. It was a thing of nightmares. Even at that distance I could see the frown lines creased into his grimy forehead, the dark little pouches of fat under his mad, black button eyes, and the sprayed spittle that accompanied his curses.

The Capri's window lost the contest with Nick's fist. I heard the glue give and the window clatter out against the side of the car and down, onto the torn grass behind us. Out of the corner of my eye I saw Sharon turn to grab at Nick as he climbed up to squeeze his way out of the opening thus provided. He must have kicked her aside; she faced forward again, nursing a bruised wrist, and Nick shouted at his father as he bounced off the side of the car and landed rolling on the ground behind us. I hit the brakes and spun the wheel with the skid, hoping to keep the Capri between Nick and Django. I didn't quite make it. He rolled to the right while I was skidding to the left, and between us we ended with Nick in the open, defenseless.

His shout was enough to distract Django from his daughters. Before Nick had recovered his footing, Django had turned the .38 on him. He got off a couple of wild shots, decided the Lincoln's window frame was in his way, and paused long enough to shove the door all the way open so he could get better aim at his son. The swans on the pond lifted their wings in ponderous alarm and fled in a splashy rustle of feathers and water. The Capri came to rest a good ten feet from the Lincoln. As a barrier between Nick and his father, it wouldn't have been worth much even if I had managed to place it as I meant to; Nick raced straight past us, arms waving, still shouting, intentionally and successfully drawing Django's fire.

I had my door open and the .22 out of my purse before the dust settled around us. Django had a clear shot at Nick. There was no time for me to get out of the car, or even to aim. I rested my arms through the window frame, squeezed the trigger, and shouted at Nick to take cover, though I didn't really suppose he would. I didn't really suppose anything; there wasn't time. Django hadn't noticed me before I fired, but he noticed me after. I thought irrelevantly how sweet and cool the scent of muddy water was, noticeable even over the burnt odor of heated car engines and cordite. The Capri's open door wasn't much of a shield against a .38; fortunately, Django was too enraged to aim.

"Give it up, Django!" My voice cracked. Getting shot at, even by someone whose aim is as bad as Django's was, is just not one of my favorite activities. "You can't win!" He could, of course, but maybe he didn't know that.

Sharon had edged open the door on her side, but Nick and the bulk of the Lincoln were between her and Django. I thought for a moment she was going to climb out into his line of fire to get a shot at him, but she thought better of it and kept down behind her door while she got to her feet and edged out and back, probably hoping to work her way across to the Lincoln and around it, to a spot where she could get a shot a Django. I didn't think she could make it without drawing his attention, but to give her a chance I threw another shot into the Lincoln.

Django responded promptly. His bullet whined past me, too close for comfort. Just the one; if I had any hope of getting him to empty the .38 in a fit of pique so we could tackle him, I lost it then. He was choosing his shots sparingly, if not well. I ducked down behind the car door and considered our options. There didn't seem to be a lot of options to consider. Django had the advantage; he knew what was going on, and he didn't care who got hurt. Two points in his favor, none in ours. Maybe we had God on our side, but if so, She wasn't proving altogether useful.

Lela and Sonja had finally reached the top of the bank and the edge of the sparse and manicured forest. Instead of escaping into its secret shadows, they stopped there in the crushed oxalis, still in easy range of Django's .38, to watch what happened behind them. That was the first good view I got of Lela's face. It was just possible to tell, through the purple mass of bruises, that without them she would be a very pretty girl.

Django, in his eagerness to destroy me and his son, still had not forgotten his daughters. He kept glancing over his shoulder in an evident agony of rage and frustration: so many people to kill, and so little time in which to do it.

I didn't want to kill anybody. I aimed the .22 to the right of Django's ear and the bullet shattered the rearview mirror inside the car. I couldn't see where Sharon had got to, and I didn't want his attention to wander. I still didn't have any effective cover against a .38, so I crouched behind what I had and shouted at him, as much to encourage myself as to discourage him. "Django, I don't want to hurt you. Give it up, and we can all still walk away from this. Let the girls go." I raised my head to peer through the open window. Django was carefully leveling the .38 at me. If I didn't kill him now, I wouldn't get another chance.

A .22 is a pitiable weapon against a mountain of flesh like that. But a .22 was all I had. He was taking his time, making sure his aim would be good, for a change. I wished he wouldn't do that.

At that distance, I didn't see how he could miss if he put some thought into it. There wasn't time to level my own weapon, to make sure of the shot, so I did the next-best thing: an instant before he fired, I dived away from the Capri and rolled as I landed, presenting a moving target, and came up firing.

Usually I'm good at instinctive shots like that. I should have hit him, and I should have kept on hitting him. Even with a .22, I might have stopped him. I didn't. My first shot missed him entirely, and there was no time for a second. Nick got in my way.

He had been hiding behind the Lincoln. When he saw his father turning away from him to follow my motion with the .38, he went over the back of the Lincoln in a flying tackle that caught Django in the chest with Nick's full body weight and all the momentum of his leap. They both went down hard against the Lincoln's open door. Django kept his grip on the revolver. He moved as though Nick were a minor inconvenience, nothing more. He used his gun hand to brace himself and the other massive arm to brush Nick off his chest the way I might brush away an insect.

The blow caught Nick on the side of the head and knocked him against the Lincoln, leaving him dazed and defenseless at his father's feet. At the top of the saffron and emerald slope above them, Lela screamed Nick's name and started back down toward the cars, her crimson skirt swirling around her, but she didn't get far; in her panic, she forgot to let go of the suitcase she and Sonja held between them. Sonja didn't let go, either.

For one confused instant they played tug-of-war with it, Sonja bracing her feet among the brittle oxalis stems and clinging for dear life, and Lela trying mindlessly to get away from her without any understanding of what held her back. I don't think she ever did realize what was happening. Instead, she lost her footing and instinct took over, making her let go of the handle to save herself from sliding back down that brightly carpeted slope.

At the last instant before Lela let go, the suitcase burst open. Sonja still had her grip on the handle. The sudden lack of resistance left her off balance. She went sprawling backward, arms flailing, among crushed leaves and blossoms. That sent the contents of the suitcase flying. Bundles of paper money spilled out at Sonja's feet and tumbled like dark green blocks down the battered slope toward the pond. No wonder Sonja hadn't wanted to let go.

Some of the bundles broke open as they fell, so that crisp bills cascaded down the slope like a dull, dry waterfall. We all watched it as though it were the most fascinating event in the universe. That kept Django from shooting Nick, which was good. It also kept me from shooting Django, which was not so good. I don't like to admit I was that easily distracted, that I risked at least Nick's life and possibly all our lives, just for the chance to watch a bunch of paper money slide down a hill.

Sharon was the first to recover her senses. She had worked her way to the back of the Lincoln, but had not been able to get nearer Django without exposing herself to his gunfire, and from where she was, she couldn't shoot him without endangering Nick. She moved while Django's attention was still on the money. Ducking down behind the bulk of the Lincoln, she edged around toward the front in the hope of getting behind Django.

It was a good move, but it didn't work. Some sound she made dragged Django's attention from the money. He saw what she was doing and, in his fury, kicked his son aside with one of those heavy, well-tended boots and propelled himself bodily away from the Lincoln. The move was so unexpected he caught us both by surprise. He had been staying so close to that car door that I think I had imagined he was physically connected to it. He aimed the .38 at me and looked at Sharon. We were both exposed, and the dinky little guns in our hands weren't a match for his. If either of us had fired, it would have had to be a hell of a shot to stop him before he could kill one or both of us.

"Drop your guns," he said. Neither of us did, but we didn't shoot, either. He looked at me, his piggy eyes calculating, and slowly lowered his weapon to cover Nick, who was still sprawled in the dusty grass by the Lincoln, dazed from being knocked against the car and kicked aside. "Drop them, or I'll kill him."

I hesitated, staring. "Why, Django? Why would you kill your own son?"

He shrugged massively, without interest, as though I had asked him why the Earth is round. "He is of no importance. Kill him, don't kill him, what's the difference, eh? Drop your guns and go away now, *gajende*. You're not wanted here."

"I won't let you kill your children."

He laughed. It was a harsh, barking sound, unaccustomed and unamused. "They are all thieves, like *gadje*. They steal from their own father. Go away."

I shook my head. "No." Nick's scalp was torn, half his face covered with streaming blood, and he clearly did not know what was going on. There was no hope he would make his own way out from under his father's gun. The heady perfume of lavender hung over the tiny clearing, stronger even than the dry scent of sunbaked earth and the cool, damp odor of the pond. A lone seagull screamed somewhere in the distance, a rusty sound like a creaking gate. I swallowed dust and said cautiously, "Nick didn't steal anything from you, did he?"

"Drop the gun, *gadjo*." He aimed another kick at Nick.

I put the gun down, but I kept talking. "And I don't think the girls did, either. That money up there is Sonja's isn't it? From the *hukkaben* in Chicago? Why do you say she's stealing it from you?" Sharon still had her gun, for all the good that did us. Django seemed to have forgotten her for the moment.

"What do you know of these things?" He kicked Nick again, catching him in the ribs this time. I might as well have kept my gun. Putting it down had delayed his abuse of Nick, but not prevented it. "This," he said, "has it been telling you what no *gadjo* should know? What do you know of our business? What has he told you?"

Sharon was edging around the Lincoln again. I couldn't see much purpose to it. He was clearly unafraid of our weapons. Even if she got behind him he might very well not give up without a fight. One of us would have to kill him, if we could. Killing is second only to being killed on my list of things I don't like doing. "He told me enough to know the money belongs to Sonja, if it belongs to anyone," I said. "She stole it from MacMurray. That makes it hers, by your own rules, doesn't it?"

He laughed again, his glance straying toward his daughters. Lela was sitting where she had fallen, watching us with dazed, uncomprehending eyes. Sonja was crawling frantically among the crushed oxalis and morning glories, gathering up her bundles of money. "It would be hers if she had stolen it, as she should have done," Django said. "That, you understand, that would have been a good thing, a thing to be proud of, and besides, the money would then be mine because I am her father and she has no husband. But she did not steal it." He glared at me, remembering who I was. "Go away. It is not to do with you. Leave us."

I saw, then, how it must have happened. "She was going to run away with MacMurray after all, wasn't she? And you found out, and you killed him. Did you kill Nick's Auntie Tia, too? Why? Did she see you with Sonja's money?"

His thick, rubbery lips twisted in a horrible travesty of a grin. A purple vein throbbed at his temple, but his eyes were cold and calm. "I killed them, and I will kill you, if you do not go. It is my money. I will kill everyone. I want my money." There was an edge of madness in his voice and in his words, but the threat was all the more real because of it.

Nick groaned and turned his bloodied head in the dirt. The movement caught Django's attention. He looked at his son and then at me, with another humorless twisting of his lips that was meant to be a smile. Very soon now, he would begin killing his defenseless children. I knew that. There was nothing I could do to save them, and I knew that, too. I had been offered a chance to escape unmolested. I could not do it. It was illogical to stay. It would

probably prove fatal to stay. I lifted my gaze from
Nick's bruised face to Django's piggy eyes and
thought with a sinking horror at my own stubborn
idiocy that it was a lousy afternoon to die.

NINETEEN

THE CITY MIGHT have been miles away. No sound of it filtered through the serenity of the forest to disturb us. A seagull croaked somewhere far overhead, its shadow skimming across the grass and out over the pond, where a solitary swan had returned to float in silent elegance. Lela, still sitting in a welter of bright skirts and crushed oxalis, wept quietly, hopelessly. Sonja was still single-mindedly collecting her bundles of money and putting them back in the broken suitcase.

A bumblebee buzzed past my ear and away on an erratic path into the shadows. Nick had begun to struggle to his feet, awkward and uncertain like a newborn colt, as though his legs were suddenly too long for his body. Django barely noticed him now. He had turned his attention to the hillside where all that money was still scattered across the broken yellow blossoms and emerald leaves.

"Sonja!" His voice was sharp with urgency. "Bring it to me, that money. Bring it, and I will let you go. It's mine, that money."

Sonja ignored him. She did not even glance up at him. Her dark eyes were intent on her task. He would have to kill someone to separate her from that money now.

He figured that out. "I will kill your brother," he said, turning the .38 quite casually toward his son. This was it: the waiting was over. I wondered, in an abstracted and altogether disinterested way, whether it would be better to tackle him now or after he had begun to fire.

His threat had no effect on Sonja at all. She might not have heard him. He thought about that, and for a long moment I thought he would kill Nick just for the hell of it; then he turned the gun toward his daughters. "I will kill your sister." I don't know why he kept threatening the others, instead of simply killing Sonja out of hand. It didn't occur to me to wonder, at the time. Perhaps he was reluctant to kill her because of them all she was the one most like him. If that was it, it would not stay his hand forever. "She is only trouble to me, refusing to stay with her husband, who is a fine boy and who paid a good bride-price for her."

Sonja didn't react, but Lela did. She clambered to her feet, tears still streaming down that bruised little face, and stumbled toward Nick and her father. "Please," she said. "Please. Nick, please. Help me." She made an expansive, innocent gesture that should have looked overly dramatic, and didn't. "I didn't know Sonja had the money. I didn't know." Standing safe in the circle of her brother's arms, she looked at her father with wounded eyes. "Don't make me go back. I know it's wrong to leave without paying back half my bride-price, but not if they beat me, and look!" She lifted her head, the better to show off the bruises on her face, and grasped the neck of her peasant blouse as though she were going to rip it away.

"Don't." Nick tightened his arm around her shoulders. "Lela, don't. It won't do no good. He don't care."

"There are bruises," she said. "I can show you the bruises. It's not right. Don't make me go back. He hurts me. His father hurts me. Nick, help me. If I have to go back, I swear I will kill myself. I swear it."

From the looks of her, she might not have to kill herself. Her husband and his family might do it for her. But at that moment I didn't know what Nick could do to help her. Nor did he. His face was taut with rage and frustration, but he made no move that might have angered his father. If he had, it would only have got him killed.

Sharon and I had more options: Django appeared to have forgotten us for the moment. I picked up my .22 and moved carefully around the Capri and across the open ground to the Lincoln, horribly aware as I did it that he might remember us at any time, and turn that big .38 on me while I was so exposed. I couldn't run; that would surely have drawn his attention. I hardly dared to move fast, in case the motion should catch his eye. Sharon stayed where she was with her puny little handgun leveled at him, covering my long walk between cars.

The ground felt like velvet under my feet. The sky overhead was a luminous blue against which the silhouettes of thick-leaved trees formed graceful, shifting shapes in rich greens and shadows. The air stank of lavender. To this day I cannot smell it without remembering that sundrenched afternoon by the swan pond and my certainty that all of us were dead. Django moved and I froze in a moment of abject terror, not even remembering to lift the .22; like a rabbit trapped in light I stood paralyzed and waited almost patiently to die. But he was only moving toward his daughter, away from me.

I started walking again. By the time I reached the Lincoln I had even begun to breathe again. I have infinite sympathy for cowardice; it can happen to anyone. Or so I choose to think, since it can happen to me. When I gained the safe haven of the Lincoln's sturdy bulk I began to hear what Django and his offspring were saying. The roar of blood in my ears had made me deaf till then. I leaned against the sun-heated metal, though it burned my hands; I was too weak to stand without support.

"It's mine," said Sonja, crouching protectively over the suitcase while she gathered up the last few dull green blocks of money. "I worked the *hukkaben.*"

"Who got you the *gadjo* identification?" said Django. "Who found MacMurray in the first place? Who helped you in every way while you worked the *hukkaben?*"

"But I worked it." She placed the blocks carefully in the suitcase, layering them evenly and patting them now and then, as though they were living creatures under her hands.

"You worked it for the family," said Django. "It is a woman's duty to support her family. Not to run away with some *gadjo* after we help her to get his money from him."

"I loved him." She said it the way one might tell the time of day. "You shouldn't have killed him."

"He had my money." I was surprised Django defended himself from her. But it wasn't much of a defense.

"You shouldn't have killed him. You shouldn't have killed Auntie Tia. You are a *gadjo* yourself, the way you act."

"Watch what you say!" It was, perhaps, the worst insult she could have thrown at him. "I am your father. You must have respect."

She spat. I'd never before seen anyone actually spit in anger. She had finished gathering money now and stood tall and straight-backed over the suitcase, her fierce eyes challenging him. "I have no respect for you. You are nothing. You do not live the life. You should have bought Lela back from her husband. You should never have sold her to him, that monster, that creature whose whole family beats his wife, what kind of family is that to give your own daughter to?"

"Bring that money down here." Django was not to be sidetracked. "It's mine. Bring it to me."

"I will not." She lifted her chin, eyes flashing.

"Then you will die." Django laughed suddenly, wildly. "As your lover died."

Nick spoke quickly, before his father could make good on that threat. "How did you find him?" he asked, his voice mild. I wasn't sure whether he really wanted to know or only wanted to distract his father from Sonja. In either case he was taking quite a chance, drawing that madman's attention. He knew it. He had been sheltering Lela in his arms, but as he spoke he moved so that he was between her and his father. "How did you know he had the money?"

Django laughed again. It was a frightening sound, like the cry of some tormented thing. "She told me," he said.

"I didn't!" Sonja looked shocked. "I wouldn't!"

"She and that *gadjo,* they made their plans on the telephone," said Django. "I heard her. She told him to bring the money to the BART station to meet her." He laughed again, high and long. "He met me, instead!"

"You did kill him!" said Sonja. "I thought so, when I saw you stash this suitcase in your car this morning. Were you afraid to leave it at my *ofisa?* I would have found it, you understand. But from the car anyone could have taken it." Pausing, she studied him thoughtfully. "Did you really kill Auntie Tia, too?"

Django shrugged, indifferent. "She saw me return with the money. She would have had me share with the family."

"So you killed her for money, like a *gadjo,*" said Nick.

Django stared at him, his brief amusement forgotten. "I killed her. Now it is my money." He turned that implacable gaze toward Sonja and made an imperious gesture. "Bring it to me."

"I will not," said Sonja. "He was going to take me to Europe, and you killed him. You will never get the money." She stepped between him and the money as though to shield it from him with her body. It wasn't a very strong shield. Django fired once, and she crumpled without a sound, like a rag doll abandoned in the midst of play.

Sharon and I had just got in position to cover Django with nobody else in our line of fire, but I lost my cool when Sonja fell. I didn't know whether she was dead, but I did know Django was turning to shoot at Nick and Lela, and I had to stop him. The sensible thing would have been for both of us to shoot him; the .22 is feeble for a gun, but it's still a gun. We could have stopped him.

I didn't shoot. Don't ask me why. I think I went a little mad when I saw the triumphant smile with which he shot his daughter and proposed to shoot her siblings. I've never done such a stupid thing before or since, but what I did when I should have fired was leapt: I tackled him.

That put me in Sharon's way so she couldn't shoot him either. I couldn't possibly hold him; he was so huge and powerful that the full flying weight of my body didn't even overbalance him. For a long second I clung to him in a mad embrace, sickened by the ripe locker-room stink of his body and the knowledge of my own stupidity. Then my mind began to work again and I tried to get a knee in his groin.

More annoyed than angry, he swatted at me the way he had swatted at Nick when Nick tackled him, and very nearly as effectively. The blow caught the side of my head and almost dislodged me from my grip. The only thing that saved me was that he had not used the hand that held the .38; that would have knocked me silly. As it was, I had just enough strength and sense to keep clinging and kicking. Sharon shouted something at me, but I didn't hear what it was. My vision cleared quickly, but all I could see was the front of Django's shirt and a filthy section of large-pored neck. I butted him in the chin with the top of my head and kicked at his legs till I felt one toe connect hard with one of his kneecaps.

That made him angry, but I didn't give him time to vent it. He lifted his hurt leg to take the weight off it. I dropped off his chest, hooked my leg around the one he was standing on, and yanked. That overbalanced him at last. He went down roaring like an animal, arms flailing. Unfortunately, one of the flailing arms hit me. Worse, it was the one with the .38, which connected solidly with the side of my head.

I was only distantly aware of falling. There was a high, thin singing in my ears. I couldn't see. The only thing that saved my life was that I landed on his gun arm, hard and heavy enough to hold it down. He used the other to pummel me in the ribs and shoulders, wherever he could reach me. Somehow, through all that and through a sense-obscuring dizziness that threatened to drag me down into darkness, I managed to retain awareness of that .38 under me, and of the need to do something about it before he used it to do something about me. I knew I would have one chance, and only one chance. There wasn't time to plan or calculate, even if my mind had been working well enough to do either thing, which it was not. I had to stop him. If I didn't, he would sure as hell stop me.

There wasn't even time to try to get the gun out of his hand. I had lost mine somewhere along the line, and I was in Sharon's way so she couldn't use hers. My mind worked as though my wits were wrapped in cotton wool; my body felt weak and clumsy as a newborn kitten, my motions awkward and seemingly slow. I folded like a rickety lawn chair, bending Django's momentarily unresisting arm under the weight of my body, aiming the .38 at his head. I must have moved faster than I thought, because he didn't have time to realize what was happening.

The blow to my head had sent waves of darkness surging like the roar of the ocean through my mind. I was aware of a need to hurry, before I drowned in the swirling emptiness. I folded my hand around Django's, forced my finger over his on the trigger, and squeezed.

He had one brief instant in which to stare at me, one fraction of a second in which to realize what I had done. His eyes were as dark and as wild as Nick's had ever been, without any of Nick's gentleness or humanity. He opened his mouth to scream or to curse, but it was too late. He was already dead.

I saw the mouth open and close like a fish out of water; saw the dark, fawn eyes bulge in the ruined face; saw the awful, slow-motion reflex of his head jerked back and away by the impact of the bullet. It seemed to take a very long time.

I think I screamed, but the only sound I heard was a long, weak, windy howl, a whispery, meaningless whine. I wanted to tell him I was sorry. I wanted to close those horrible eyes. I wanted to turn it back into a world where Gypsies were amiable, wandering thieves and I hadn't killed anyone. I could not have what I wanted. All I could do was sit in the dirt under the unrelenting sun and stare at what I had done.

TWENTY

THE SUMMERY POTPOURRI of cut grass, damp earth, and lavender that had blessed that tiny clearing was overwhelmed now by the stink of blood and feces, the crowning indignities of death, which offend only the living. Through the eyes of the dead, I thought sensibly, nothing must look undignified. Nothing is left. The body is only a place where someone lives; when he moves out, there's nobody left to offend.

"Ailie."

Here I was having a brilliant philosophical revelation, and someone was trying to distract me. I was easily distracted. I had forgotten what the revelation was about. I turned my head carefully. It was unsteady, on a neck that seemed much too long and thin. My whole body ached, and I could not quite think why. If I were going to have philosophical revelations, perhaps I ought to have them about something closer to home. Or perhaps it would be wiser just to concentrate on breathing. It occurred to me that breathing was not the easiest thing I had ever done. It hurt. It hurt a lot. It occurred to me that I didn't like pain.

"Ailie, can you hear me?"

It was Sharon. She was dabbing at my face with a piece of torn cloth, trying to wipe away the blood. I smiled foolishly. "You're all right," I said.

Her face was pale and serious. "*I* am," she said. "What about you?"

"I'll be okay."

"You look terrible."

"Thanks a lot." The darkness was receding. I could see around us again. Sunlight still glinted on the rippled pond water and cast pillars of burnished gold down through the trees. There was a morning glory creeper under my hand, its purple trumpet folded tight against the light.

I lifted my gaze to find Sharon crouched in front of me, anxiously studying my face. I ignored her. There was something nasty I didn't want to think about. I thought about it and turned my head again.

In the dusty, clover-dotted grass beside me, Django lay staring at the sky with dead onyx eyes. The .38 was still clutched in his grubby, lifeless hand. Nick and Lela had moved as if drawn to him against their will. They stared down at him with expressionless intensity, their arms around each other like small children weathering a terrible storm. I looked at them, then up the hill where Sonja lay sprawled among the broken flowers like a forgotten toy, her face turned toward the suitcase full of neatly stacked and banded bundles of bills.

Sharon followed my gaze. "She's dead," she said, but she rose anyway and walked reluctantly up the slope to bend over that bright, limp form, making sure.

I put my head between my hands gently, as though it were extremely fragile, which was how it felt just then. The .38 had cut my scalp when Django hit me. My face must have been as bloody as Nick's; scalp wounds do bleed a lot. But the bruise it made hurt more than the cut. I felt bruised all over. I couldn't think straight. I looked up at Nick and Lela and wondered what to say to them. They seemed wholly unaware of me, so I decided not to say anything.

Sharon came back down the slope with the suitcase cradled in her arms. It seemed a small thing for people to have died over. In the aftermath of terror I could not understand the value of so abstract a thing as money. Life had always been the thing I valued most. At that moment, it was the only thing I really valued at all.

She put the suitcase down beside Django. Nick and Lela had begun to shift and adjust themselves with little muttered sounds and uncertain movements, as though they were waking from sleep. Sharon ignored them and looked at me. "You gonna be okay?"

"Told you, I'm fine." To prove it, I clambered awkwardly to my feet and stood swaying, waiting for the world to settle back into place. It showed an alarming tendency to spin and tumble, threatening to knock me off my precarious balance. My ribs and one shoulder felt as though I had been hit by a car. Django wasn't that much smaller than some cars.

Sharon was studying Nick. "You don't look so good, either," she said. "You gonna be okay?"

Nick seemed surprised. "Sure, of course I'm okay." But he touched the side of his head where Django had kicked him, and winced at the gentle pressure of his fingers. When he noticed me watching him he made an odd little gesture, half a shrug and half a nod toward his fallen father, and said, "He's done worse, before," as though that explained something.

Sharon stood still, surveying the clearing, then lifted the suitcase and gestured aimlessly with her free hand. "Murder and suicide?"

"I guess so," I said. My obsession with reporting corpses to the police had fallen by the wayside. "Only problem is the extra car tracks."

"No motive," said Sharon, looking down at the suitcase in her arms.

"No need," I said. "After all, he did shoot her. And himself. But the police will know there was another car here."

"They won't know it was ours," said Sharon. "There's nothing to connect us to them."

"Not us, maybe, but what about Nick and Lela?" If we were going to stand there in that sundrenched, stinking clearing and plan our futures, I thought we might as well plan for all of us.

Nick answered before Sharon could. "We will be gone," he said. "That money, part of it's ours." He sounded stubborn.

"All of it's yours," said Sharon, surprising him.

"Unless Django and Sonja have other heirs," I said.

"I don't understand that, heirs," said Nick. Beside him, Lela pulled a snowy white cloth from a pocket in her skirt and began to clean his face with a mother's gentle concern.

"People who inherit when they die," said Sharon.

"Like if either of them had any kids besides you," I said. "Or living parents besides him." I nodded at Django.

Nick considered that seriously. "Sonja, she didn't have no kids," he said. "And Django, he killed his except us. My mom, too, he killed her. He beat her and when she got sick he let her die." He shook his head. "There's nobody."

"Then the money's yours," I said.

"We wouldn't've got it if it weren't for you guys," he said. "If it's ours, then it belongs to all of us." He glanced at Lela for confirmation.

She nodded earnestly. "We should share it. Four ways," she said. "Okay, Nick?"

"Sure," said Nick. He smiled down at her, proud of her moral values. I saw his arm tighten across her shoulder before he turned back to us and said thoughtfully, "Lela and me, we'll pay back half her bride-price to her husband's family. Then maybe if Sonja had those airline tickets with her, maybe we could have those, too. We could go to where she was going and we'll start a new life, the two of us. We'll find Lela a real husband. Somebody who lives the life, who'll treat her right." He looked startled, then pleased. "Hell, I could even buy me a wife, if we was somewhere where nobody knows us, where my father has not poisoned the people against me." His dark eyes glistened, dreaming, perhaps, of the quality of wife he could buy with his share of one hundred thousand dollars.

"I have the airline tickets," said Lela. She smiled shyly at him. "I picked her pocket."

Nick looked at her in open admiration. "Sonja's? You picked Sonja's pocket?"

"She never knew," said Lela. "I know I shouldn't steal from family, but I didn't know what she was going to do with me, and I thought—"

Nick hugged her. "It's okay," he said. "It's okay, little one. You did good."

"That's settled, then," Sharon said with satisfaction. "Let's get out of here."

"Yes, do let's." I had not been paying close attention to the conversation. I was still dizzy and confused from Django's blows. But I understood one thing very well indeed: I wanted to leave that place. "We've stayed too long already. If anyone heard gunfire down this road, we could get trapped in here. There's no alternate way out if the police come to investigate." It was a rational excuse for my anxiety to leave. The truth was that the swan pond, with its banks of cascading flowers and its verge of emerald grass, filigreed with sunlight through resinous eucalyptus trees, would never seem as peaceful to me as it once had. I would always remember it stinking of lavender and inhabited by corpses.

No one else made a move, so I turned away and headed for the Capri, moving on unsteady legs over ground that swayed like a ship's deck.

"Couldja give us a ride to the airport?" asked Nick. To my relief, he and the others had followed me.

"You don't have any other stops to make before you leave town?" asked Sharon. I made no objection when she got in on the driver's side. I wasn't feeling very well. "I mean, don't you need to pick up your belongings somewhere?"

"We're wearing them." Nick grinned. "What you maybe don't understand, Gypsies, we don't own a lot of things."

A lawn mower began to drone in the distance. Another of the swans came waddling out of the undergrowth and plopped back into the pond with a muted splash and a nervous flutter of wings. The rest would be back soon. They were city birds, only briefly startled by loud noises. However isolated that clearing felt, it was a part of a very big and very noisy city. People die every day in the city, and not all of them die quietly. Swans don't care.

I thought that was another philosophical revelation, but when I tried to repeat it to Sharon she told me I'd feel better after I rested. She was right.

We dropped Nick and Lela at the airport. It was a long drive, but then, our share of the money was ample to pay for a lot of long drives. Even after we had paid our back rent and bought a bigger ad in next year's yellow pages, we would have a lot of money left over. Some Puritan sense of morality made me try to talk Nick and Lela into keeping more of it, but they weren't interested. They did keep the suitcase; they needed it to carry their share. How they planned to get that much cash through customs was something I didn't even ask. Doubtless Gypsies had their ways.

Sharon called Dr. Steve to tend my cuts and bruises, but I didn't really need him. I think she just wanted to tell the story to somebody who wouldn't run with it to the cops. Dr. Steve was always a good listener.

While he was there, the El Cerrito cops who had taken my .38 for ballistics tests returned it with thanks and muted apologies. They were obviously curious about my battered appearance, but they didn't ask, and I wasn't telling. We parted on amiable terms. I even had the impression that Ripple might call me sometime, for purely personal reasons.

Smiling to myself when they had gone, I put away the .38 and gave Sharon back her .22, poured us all some Boodles gin to celebrate, and settled in my most comfortable chair to listen to Sharon tell Dr. Steve how we happened to get rich that day. Late afternoon sunlight glittering with dust motes splashed broad copper bands across my carpet. Out on the bay, the foghorns sang their warnings over the water: the heat wave was ending at last. There was a fog-bank rolling in low through the Golden Gate again.

REGINALD HILL

SINGING
THE
SADNESS

Private Investigator Joe Sixsmith, who has the uncanny ability to be in the wrong place at the wrong time, rushes into a burning cottage to save a young woman trapped inside. While he earns a hero's status and a few blisters, the woman isn't so lucky. She's barely alive, nameless...and the subject of Joe's new mystery.

Joe is in Wales for a church choir festival, but now his vocal chords are too singed for singing. He's been retained by two very interested parties to uncover the identity of the young woman, a trail that threatens to reveal dark secrets, scandal and sordid doings behind closed doors of the small town of Llanffugiol.

Available January 2001 at your favorite retail outlet.

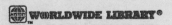

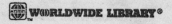